THE
CHARCOAL ENIGMA

A Journey to Life's Ultimate Secret

ECHO SABLE

TABLE OF CONTENTS

CHAPTER 1

Gold for Charcoal

A cryptic advertisement surfaced in the morning paper, almost as if it had slipped through the cracks of reality: "A piece of charcoal for sale. Previously offered price accepted. Call 181524271215 if interested."

I missed this peculiar offer entirely, but my friend didn't.

A fervent admirer of fantasy novels and a self-proclaimed intellect, he had a knack for detecting the extraordinary in the mundane. He spotted the ad on its debut and called me that very afternoon.

When I picked up, a bizarre, gravelly voice greeted me, dripping with mischief: "Ash, guess who I am?"

I chuckled, caught between irritation and amusement. "Get lost. Who else could it be but you, you idiot?"

The voice dropped its act, revealing the familiar timbre of Harlan. "Haha, you'll never guess it was me!"

"Apologies," I retorted, "but the idiot I referred to was indeed you."

Harlan's voice cut through the line, sharp and defiant. "You can't fool me! You may call everyone an idiot, but you didn't guess it was me. Let's break it down: First, I rarely call you. Second, I've never played the 'guess who' game on the phone before. Third, my voice just now was deliberately disguised, and I always project sincerity. Given these facts, there's no way you could have guessed it was me."

His mock-serious logic was infuriating and ridiculous. I snapped, "Get to the point, Harlan. No one wants to indulge your tedious games!"

Momentarily taken aback, he finally spoke, his voice tinged with hurt, "Alright, no need to get angry. What do you think of that ad?"

"What ad?" I replied, genuinely puzzled.

"Aha!" he exclaimed, "Your brain's gone soft! An ad like that would have piqued your curiosity years ago, but now..."

I cut him off, "Just tell me about the ad."

He laughed, "I won't. Consider it a test of your deductive skills. What paper do I read? Why didn't you see it?"

Fed up, I slammed the phone down, refusing to engage in his charade. Surely, he'd call back to spill the details. But the phone stayed silent.

I turned my attention to sorting books, purging unwanted volumes from my study and relegating them to the trash by the back door.

The sun was dipping below the horizon, casting long shadows across my quiet retreat. I set aside the well-worn pages of an old book and turned, only to be confronted by the blinding glare of headlights bearing down on me with relentless speed.

The road behind my home was ordinarily silent, a forgotten path leading to ancient stone steps that descended perilously down the mountain. Yet now, it was alive with unfolding chaos. The car's trajectory seemed driven by madness or desperation—either it intended to end my life or sought its own demise.

In the instant realization struck, I screamed, pivoting swiftly to evade the oncoming vehicle.

It careened past, a tempest of metal and velocity, catching my coat in its wake. My heart pounded as I watched it race toward the precipice, brakes shrieking in defiance.

The car spun wildly, a dervish of momentum, before it halted precariously at the edge.

In the chaos, I had failed to glimpse the driver. Now, as the dust settled, my anger simmered, eyes fixed on the silent vehicle.

The door flung open, and a figure emerged, tumbling onto the ground. He staggered upright, eyes wide, breath ragged, face a mask of terror. His identity eluded me until he cried out, "Oh my God! Ash!"

Recognition dawned—Harlan. A mix of anger and wry amusement bubbled within as I approached. "What are you doing? Planning to kill someone, or is this a suicide attempt?"

As I drew near, he reached out, clutching my arm with the desperation of a man overboard, clinging to driftwood.

While Harlan often carried an air of nervous mystery, this time was different. His terror was palpable, his demeanor uncharacteristically shaken. It was clear that he wasn't putting on a show—something truly extraordinary had rattled him to his core, leaving him visibly horrified. Whatever he had encountered must have been beyond the ordinary, pushing him to the brink of fear.

Seeing this, my ire softened, giving way to concern. "What's going on? Take your time and explain."

In fact, at this moment, even if I asked him to speak quickly, he couldn't say anything because he was just constantly panting, his face turning pale.

I reached out, gently patting his shoulder to steady him. After what felt like an eternity, he regained his composure enough to whisper, "What did I do just now?"

I gestured to my torn shirt, a testament to the near-tragedy. "You almost hit me, and then you nearly plunged down the stone steps to your death!"

His eyes widened with a fresh wave of shock, scanning the deserted street with a nervous energy that was contagious. Despite the stillness around us, an inexplicable tension filled the air, setting my own nerves on edge.

"Let's go inside and talk," he insisted between gasps.

Once inside, he clung to my arm until the door clicked shut behind us. Only then did he release his grip, exhaling a deep sigh of relief. I poured him a glass of wine, which he downed in a single gulp, before fixing me with an intense stare. "That advertisement!"

The mention of an advertisement left me baffled. I had long forgotten any such thing, its details lost to the recesses of my mind. "Oh, that ad," I replied, feigning understanding.

Harlan poured himself another drink, quaffing it with urgency. "Don't you think this ad is strange?"

I shrugged, confessing my ignorance. "Honestly, I've been so busy. I don't even know what ad you're talking about."

Harlan's eyes were wide with a mix of urgency and bewilderment, as if he'd stumbled upon something otherworldly. I tried to lighten the mood, offering a smile. "You always did have a knack for getting worked up. I can't dig through old papers just because of your strange phone call."

But his insistence was unwavering. "No need for old newspapers—it's right there in today's edition!"

I settled into my chair, reaching for the newspaper resting on the table. "Alright, show me where this advertisement is."

Harlan took a seat across from me, his demeanor tense. "Page three of the classified ads, in the transfer column."

As I flipped to the section he indicated, I couldn't help but wonder what had caught his attention. Classified ads were often a forgotten corner of the paper unless you had a specific reason to look. Yet, he'd found something in this mundane space that seemed to grip him with unease. The advertisement was indeed small, almost unnoticeable, with a peculiar message: "A piece of charcoal for sale——"

I furrowed my brow, perplexed. The idea of selling charcoal in a newspaper ad was absurd. The cost of the ad itself could buy several kilograms of charcoal. Clearly, the ad was a guise, a riddle spun from mundane threads. Even the phone number was a farce, a twelve-character string that belonged nowhere in the world.

I met his gaze. "Yes, it's odd. But surely not odd enough to drive you to such extremes."

Harlan's voice rose in protest. "I wasn't trying to commit suicide!"

"But the way you drove——" I began, only to be cut off.

"Listen to me!" he implored, his urgency impossible to ignore.

The advertisement had undoubtedly caught the eye of many, sparking curiosity with its oddity. Yet, for most, it remained a passing peculiarity—nothing more than a strange blip in their day. But Harlan had clearly been compelled to dig deeper, driven by more than mere curiosity.

"What did you do after seeing this advertisement?" I inquired, curiosity piqued.

"First, I reasoned that charcoal, having no real value, was a code," Harlan explained, regaining his composure. His confidence returned as I nodded in agreement. "Secondly, while it appeared to be an ad, it was actually a message between two parties."

I murmured my assent, though I remained skeptical. He pressed on, eager to elaborate. "Consider the phrase 'Price is negotiable.' Imagine a person, A, who has something to sell. A has been in contact with a buyer, but the deal fell through. After some time, A decides to reopen negotiations, so this ad serves as a signal to previous buyers."

I clapped him on the knee. "Impressive! Your deductive skills have really sharpened."

Harlan beamed with pride. "Curiosity got the better of me, and I wanted to know what 'charcoal' symbolized, so I called the number."

I blinked. "Hold on, how did you manage to dial a twelve-digit number?"

With a sly grin, Harlan revealed the trick. "Just a bit of creative thinking and voilà!"

I groaned inwardly—his penchant for cryptic answers was back. If he could figure it out, surely I could too. I scrutinized the twelve-digit string, knowing our local numbers were only six digits. It clicked: every two digits were divisible by three, transforming into a single digit, revealing the true six-digit number.

"Ah, divide every two digits by three, and there's the phone number," I said, feeling a sense of triumph.

Harlan gave me an appraising look. "You figured it out faster than I did—it took me an entire hour."

I waved away the compliment. "So, you called. What happened next?"

His smile turned rueful. "Now I deeply regret my curiosity. I've landed myself in a mess!"

I arched an eyebrow. "A brush with the underworld?"

Harlan shook his head, a shadow of doubt clouding his features, and said, "I'm not sure. I managed to crack the code to the right phone number and, in my excitement, dialed it immediately. The line rang endlessly before an elderly voice, frail yet firm, answered. 'Who are you looking for?' she inquired. I responded eagerly, 'Are you selling charcoal? I'm interested!' There was a pause, a muted exchange as if she were conferring with someone nearby. Then, she asked, 'Do you agree with the price?'"

I studied Harlan intently as he offered a wry smile, tinged with regret. "In hindsight, hanging up would have been wise, but I was caught in the thrill of the moment. 'I agree,' I said."

Curiosity piqued, I interrupted, "What was the price?"

Harlan chuckled ruefully. "That was the very question I asked myself. What was the price? Money? Knowing the price would unlock the enigma of what this 'charcoal' truly represented. Yet, I couldn't outright ask; a genuine buyer would already know. Prices, after all, is as previously offered.

"You could have approached it indirectly," I suggested.

He slapped the armrest with sudden realization. "Precisely. I posed, 'I agree to the price, but what's the mode of payment? Cash or check?'"

I couldn't help but grin. "Clever move."

His eyes narrowed at me, "Clever, yes, but risky. The old woman's voice cut through the line, 'Gold! The same volume as the charcoal!'"

My eyebrows shot up in surprise. Harlan and I exchanged bewildered glances, both grappling with the cryptic notion of exchanging charcoal for gold by volume.

"It's bizarre," I mused. "Charcoal and gold, both measured by volume—it defies logic!"

Harlan nodded, recalling his astonishment. "That price only deepened my curiosity. Instinctively, I blurted, 'Alright,

I'll bring the gold. Where to exchange the goods?' I deliberately phrased it as 'exchange goods' to hint that I understood the charcoal was merely a facade. The old woman, unfazed, simply replied, 'The old place.'"

I chuckled, "You've got yourself a conundrum. How do you know where 'the old place' is?"

He sighed, "Indeed, I didn't. But I was quick on my feet. I improvised, 'The old place won't work. Let's meet by the park fountain at four this afternoon.'"

I frowned skeptically, "The park fountain? Harlan, this isn't a date. This deal is shrouded in mystery."

He shrugged defiantly, "You have to suggest decisively to deter her from insisting on the old place. Do you have a better idea?"

"Over three thousand," I scoffed, "but I doubt she'd accept your proposal."

His grin was triumphant. "Wrong! She agreed."

I blinked in disbelief. "Really? Did you meet the mysterious seller?"

Harlan nodded, his silence louder than any words he could muster.

I glanced at the clock, its hands inching past five. Harlan and I had been engrossed in our conversation for the better part of twenty minutes. He had burst in around four-fifteen, a tempest of urgency and dread. The drive from the park to my place spanned only ten minutes, a brief passage of time that belied the gravity etched on his pale, stricken face. This meant whatever transpired during his four o'clock meeting had left an indelible mark, compelling him to rush here in a state of shock.

I drew a deep breath, steadying myself for the revelation. "Was the appointment as dreadful as it seems?"

Harlan's breath hitched, a reflexive gasp escaping his lips as he nodded, a silent testament to the horror of the encounter. "Tell me everything," I urged, leaning in, eager to unravel the layers of this cryptic and ominous tale.

As I spoke, I stood and poured Harlan another glass of wine, hoping it might steady his nerves. He took the glass, turning it thoughtfully in his hands. "After hanging up the phone, I prepared to leave. I didn't have any gold to offer, but that was irrelevant. My objective was to uncover what they intended to exchange. The whole affair reeked of something illicit, cloaked in secrecy. I suspected it might involve a crime, so I braced for the unexpected. I drove there and parked as close to the fountain as I could."

He gestured toward the ashtray on the table. "This represents the fountain," he said, then placed the glass a short distance away. "And this is where I parked, about 100 meters off. I arrived early, at 3:50, and remained in the car, watching the fountain for any sign of the other party."

"Smart move," I commended him. "If they turned out to be dangerous, you could have driven off immediately!"

Harlan let out a weary sigh. "Even if they weren't outright hostile, I wouldn't risk getting out if they looked troublesome. But—" He paused, his voice tinged with hesitation. "There weren't many people around the fountain, just a few scattered souls who clearly weren't my contact. So, I waited. At 3:58, I spotted an old woman with a square cloth bag, scanning the area as she approached the fountain. Instantly, I knew she was the one."

I chuckled lightly. "An old woman? Did you think she'd be easy to handle?"

He spread his hands, dismissing my jest. "It was just an old woman; there was no reason to fear. I exited the car and approached. By the time I reached the fountain, she was seated, and I strolled by, feigning nonchalance, scrutinizing her intently."

"You could do that because she assumed the caller was the buyer from a previous, uncompleted transaction—not a stranger. You were invisible to her."

"Exactly," Harlan agreed. "She barely glanced at me, giving me the perfect opportunity to observe her. But the more I watched, the stranger she seemed."

"Was she a witch-like figure?" I teased.

He practically shouted in response, "Absolutely not!"

"Whoa, calm down," I laughed. "Why the intensity?"

"Because you're completely off base. She was over seventy, dressed in a black satin gown and matching coat, adorned with a large but yellowed pearl necklace. Her hair was silvery, her demeanor serene, exuding an indefinable aura—not one you'd associate with your average nouveau riche."

I nodded thoughtfully. "You're suggesting she came from a distinguished background?"

"Indeed," Harlan affirmed. "Her attire and bearing spoke volumes. As I passed her, I thought to myself, perhaps I shouldn't meddle with such an old lady. I considered being straightforward. Yet, the package she held caught my eye, and I was perplexed all over again."

I took a sip of wine, intrigued. "What was so peculiar about the package?"

Harlan continued, "The package was wrapped in dark purple satin, adorned with intricately embroidered flowers. Despite its age, the quality of the embroidery was unmistakable, the kind one doesn't typically see in modern urban settings."

I nodded, "Older generations often hold on to nostalgic items. It's not uncommon."

"True," he conceded. "But what struck me was the size— about 30 centimeters square."

"You mentioned it was square. I suspect there's a box inside that satin."

"Exactly," Harlan affirmed. "I suspected as much. But the 'charcoal', if it's housed in such a sizable box, must occupy quite some space. Remember, she said over the phone, 'The price of a piece of charcoal is the same volume of gold.'"

I chuckled, "A large box can hold something very small, after all."

He shot me a sharp look. "If it's small and takes up little space, it might be more valuable than gold! Have you considered that?"

His retort left me momentarily speechless. "Well, it's unlikely there's just a piece of charcoal in there," I countered.

"That's precisely what's puzzling," Harlan said, deep in thought. "I felt compelled to discover the box's contents. So, I approached her and declared, 'Old lady, I am the one you're waiting for.' She looked up, eyes scrutinizing me, and asked, 'Why is it you? Who are you to him?'"

I grimaced, sensing the awkwardness of the situation. The "he" she referred to was likely the previous potential buyer. Her advertisement targeted specifically at him, not expecting an outsider might intrude out of curiosity.

"I didn't falter and said," Harlan recounted. "'He's unavailable, so I'm here in his stead.' The old woman seemed displeased but didn't protest further. She scrutinized me and asked, 'Didn't you say you'd bring gold? Where is it?' I replied, 'I can't exactly carry it around openly!'"

Harlan paused, sipping his wine with a rueful smile. "I thought I'd given a proper response. Even if it were 100 taels of gold, I could carry it discreetly. But the moment I said it, her expression darkened, and she stood, declaring, 'Don't lie, the gold isn't with you!'"

I looked at him, intrigued. "How did she see through your bluff so quickly?"

"I didn't understand then, but it became clear soon after."

He continued, "I conceded, 'Fine, it's not with me. It's in the car.' I pointed to the car. Her expression turned somber, and I grew uneasy. I ventured, 'May I see the charcoal?'"

He took another deep sip, the memory clearly weighing on him. "I expected her to refuse flatly. But to my surprise, she sighed, 'We need the money, hence the sale, though I'm loath to part with it.' With that, she began to unwrap the satin, revealing a box—a beautifully crafted, gold-painted lacquer box, exquisite and inlaid with mother-of-pearl. As the box emerged, she produced a set of keys. The lock was an ancient Chinese design, and the keyring held several keys meant for such locks. She swiftly selected the appropriate key and inserted it into the lock—"

I waved my hand, cutting through the suspense. "Enough with the buildup. What's in the box? A human head?"

Harlan's eyes widened with a mix of disbelief and exasperation. "If it were a human head, I might not be as shocked!"

"Then, what is it?" I pressed.

He replied loudly, "A piece of charcoal!"

I blinked, incredulous. "A piece of charcoal? You—are you sure you saw it clearly?"

"Absolutely," he affirmed. "What else could it be? It's just a piece of charcoal. Anyone could see that plainly."

I jumped in, "How big was it?"

Harlan described it, "A fairly large piece, square, about 20 centimeters on each side — a substantial chunk of charcoal."

"Hmm," I mused. "I figured it must be sizeable for her to instantly realize you weren't carrying the equivalent volume in gold."

"Exactly," he nodded. "The moment I saw this hefty piece of charcoal, I realized that swapping it for the same volume of gold would mean over 100 kilograms! The old lady must be out of her mind. How could a piece of charcoal warrant such an exchange? I exclaimed, 'It's really just a piece of charcoal!' The old lady snapped back, 'Of course, it's a piece of charcoal!' I reached out to grab it, and as soon as I did, she smacked my hand, causing the charcoal to drop back into the box. She gave me a shove that sent me stumbling backward."

I interjected, "Hold on! You weigh at least 60 kilograms. How did an old lady manage to push you back?"

"Yes," he admitted sheepishly, "maybe I was caught off guard, or perhaps she was surprisingly strong."

I frowned, a thought nagging at the edges of my mind, but I kept it to myself. Harlan continued, "As I stepped back, she slammed the lid shut. I pointed at the box, insisting, 'Old lady, that's just a piece of charcoal!' Having held it briefly, I was certain. She demanded, 'Who are you?' I tried to explain, but before I could speak, I felt my arms being bound from behind."

I sat up straight, the gravity of the situation sinking in. Harlan's curiosity had led him straight into trouble. The other party must have realized he wasn't their intended contact and sent the old lady with a genuine piece of charcoal to throw him off. What initially seemed like a mysterious, clandestine deal had now taken a darker turn. His curiosity had come with a price, and now it seemed he was about to pay it.

Harlan panted heavily, his eyes wide with lingering fear. "The man who grabbed me was incredibly strong. I struggled, but it was useless. Then, I felt a sharp pain as he kneed me in the tailbone. It was excruciating, tears sprang to my eyes."

I nodded, understanding the severity. "He must have been a martial arts expert, targeting your vital points. A bit more force, and you could have been paralyzed."

"Don't scare me like that!" Harlan exclaimed. "I screamed in pain. The old lady ordered, 'Let him go. He's just a curious fool who saw our ad.' But the voice behind me insisted, 'We can't just let him off!' Yet, the old lady was firm, 'Let him go!' Reluctantly, the man released me with a forceful shove that sent me stumbling forward until I fell. As I pushed himself up, I caught sight of my assailant."

His face turned ashen as he relived the terror. "I saw him..."The fear in his eyes made me uneasy. "Who was it?" I prompted.

Harlan swallowed hard, the sound audible in the silence. "He—he only had half a face!" he finally blurted out, his voice a mix of horror and disbelief.

I blinked, trying to process this bizarre revelation. "Half a face?" It was such an odd description that I was momentarily at a loss.

He repeated, breathless, "Don't you get it? He only has half a face!"

I shook my head, bewildered. "I don't understand."

Grabbing the wine bottle, he took a large swig, gesturing to his own face. "He—only has half a face. One side is normal, the other side—nothing."

I interrupted, "So, you mean one side of his face is intact, but the other is missing entirely?"

Harlan seemed frustrated, "Exactly! One side looks ordinary. The other side is completely gone."

I tried to clarify, but his agitation grew. "Are you saying he's missing half of his facial features, like the eyes and nose on one side? Or is it like half his head is missing?"

His anger flared, "Stop it! You're making it more confusing!"

I chuckled, half in frustration, half in disbelief. "You saw him, yet you can't describe him properly?"

"Who would scrutinize someone with only half a face like that?" he snapped.

Despite his explanations, I still found it hard to visualize this "half-faced" individual, and Harlan's continued distress made it clear he couldn't either. I decided to change tack.

"Alright, let's set that aside for now. What did you do next, after seeing him?"

Harlan sighed heavily, the weight of the memory pressing on him. "Naturally, I ran. He was terrifying! I felt my heart pounding, ready to leap out of my chest. I scrambled to my feet and dashed for the car. The whole time, he was laughing—a horrible sound—and chasing me!"

I said, trying to inject some logic, "If you had kept your cool, you might have realized he wasn't actually going to harm you. After all, they did let you go."

Harlan glared at me, incredulous. "Keep calm? With a half-faced man chasing you? Could you stay calm?"

Even now, I couldn't quite grasp the image of this "half-faced" man. Harlan's inability to provide a clear description left me perplexed, but I couldn't press further.

"So then, what did you do next?" I asked, hoping to steer the conversation back to something less bewildering.

Harlan recounted with a tremor in his voice, "I got into the car and started it up. As I was driving away, that man— the one with half a face—somehow managed to latch onto the car and stick his head in through the window."

As he described this, Harlan leaned in, his face mere inches from mine, mirroring the terrifying proximity he had experienced. His expression was a mixture of fear and disbelief.

I nodded, piecing together the scene in my mind. "So, he was as close to you as you are to me right now?"

Harlan pulled back, sitting upright, and nodded solemnly.

"You must have gotten a good look at him then," I suggested.

He shouted in exasperation, "I've already told you what he looked like! He was—"

I cut him off, finishing for him, "He only had half a face."

Harlan glared at me, a mix of frustration and resignation in his eyes. "What happened after that?" I prompted.

"What else could I do?" he said with a hint of desperation. "I closed my eyes and refused to look at him!"

I was startled. "You were driving!"

"Yes, at high speed," he admitted. "I closed my eyes and just barreled forward. Of course, I peeked occasionally. The first time I opened my eyes, he was gone. I don't know when he left. But I was terrified he'd come back, so I kept opening and closing my eyes all the way to your place."

I stood up, understanding now why he had nearly run me over upon arrival. "You're lucky to be alive! Driving like that—you could have killed someone, or yourself!"

Harlan stood as well, moving closer to me. He took a deep breath and whispered conspiratorially, "Ash, I don't think this person is from Earth."

Hearing that, I couldn't help but laugh internally. The notion seemed absurd, yet there was a part of me that found it intriguing. After all, "not from Earth" was a phrase that often danced on the edge of my own musings.

CHAPTER 2

The Once Glorious Charcoal Gang

Of course, I don't deny the possibility of extraterrestrial beings among us. In fact, I'm quite convinced of their presence. However, in the strange tale Harlan spun, I couldn't see any evidence suggesting the "half-faced man" hailed from beyond Earth.

Despite my inability to clearly visualize this mysterious figure, one thing was evident: his prowess in Chinese martial arts. Harlan, a thrill-seeker himself, had trained in various disciplines such as kendo, judo, karate, and taekwondo. Yet, he was subdued in an instant. The precision strike to his spine—a vulnerable nexus of nerves—was a classic move from Chinese martial arts, something I doubted an alien would master.

So, when he floated the alien theory, I waved it off. "Enough with the nonsense! There aren't that many aliens running around."

Harlan blinked, perplexed. "Then who is he? And why does he only have half a face?"

I countered, "And the old lady? Does she have only half a face too?"

He grew agitated. "The old lady is just a regular person. She must be under the control of the half-faced alien!"

I chuckled. "That can't be it. You said yourself the half-faced man obeyed her orders and let you go. Clearly, she's in charge."

His theory faltered, Harlan looked sheepish but persisted. "I've handed you such a mystery, yet you're not curious to investigate?"

I pondered his tale. "Are you absolutely sure it was just charcoal?"

"Of course! I know what charcoal looks like," he insisted.

I fell silent, turning over the oddities in my mind. Why was this piece of charcoal valued at its volume in gold? What was its significance? Moreover, someone was willing to negotiate for it—suggesting a previous offer had been made and rejected.

Lost in thought, I found no immediate solution. Harlan prodded, "Aren't you going to do something?"

"Without a solid lead, what can I do?"

He shouted, "What's wrong with you? You have a phone number, use it!"

I laughed, "And end up like you, setting up a meeting only to flee?"

Frustrated, he snapped, "Fine, if you won't help, I will. That half-faced man isn't from Earth, and I intend to find out where he is from!"

He threw down the gauntlet, "Ash, once I crack this, dealing with aliens won't just be your domain!"

I was amused. "I never claimed exclusivity, and there's no need to challenge me."

After another sip of wine, he studied me. I feigned disinterest, prompting him to sigh, "Alright, I'll pursue this on my own."

"Good luck," I replied coolly.

At the door, he paused, and I said, "Remember, a phone number can be as good as an address."

He retorted, "I know that!"

I added, "This seems more like a crime than a mystery. It doesn't involve you, yet you're diving in headfirst. Tread carefully."

My caution was genuine, but he scoffed. "You sound jealous! Don't worry, I'm committed."

I shrugged. I'd done my part as a friend. If he chose not to heed my warning, there was little more I could do.

* * *

That evening, as twilight settled over the city, Flora returned home. After a simple dinner, we settled into the comfortable routine of reading the newspaper. The air was filled with the warmth of casual conversation, and I was on the verge of broaching a certain topic when Flora, with an unexpected urgency, jabbed a finger at the newspaper. "Look at this," she exclaimed, her voice tinged with curiosity. "This advertisement is peculiar. Have you noticed it?"

I chuckled, the sound echoing softly in the room. "What is it? Another sale on charcoal?"

Flora nodded, her expression knitted with intrigue as she scrutinized the long string of digits—the phone number— printed in the advertisement.

"Do you have any idea what this so-called 'charcoal' costs?" I asked, my tone teasing.

She flashed a knowing smile, her eyes dancing with mischief. "Of course, it's not actual charcoal. It's a code—a cipher for something else entirely!"

I shook my head, enjoying the playful banter. "You're mistaken. It really is charcoal."

Flora's gaze met mine, a glimmer of challenge in her eyes. "Have you unraveled the mystery of the phone number and dialed it?"

I leaned back, savoring the moment. "Not I, but Harlan did. Do you remember him?"

Flora leaned back, her eyes narrowing with the precision of a master strategist. "Remember," she began, "he possesses an uncanny knack for deduction. This phone number—it strikes me as a cipher of sorts. Consider it: each two-digit segment divisible by three, no?"

I applauded her insight with a few enthusiastic claps. "Exactly! And speaking of enigmas, do you want to hear Harlan's latest escapade? It's quite the tale!"

Flora, momentarily distracted, lowered her newspaper, casting a sidelong glance my way before dismissing my enthusiasm with a wave. "I don't think so. If it were as fascinating as you claim, you wouldn't be idling at home after hearing his story."

I leaned in, earnest, "Oh, but it truly is remarkable! I refrained from joining him on his latest investigation because he suspected an extraterrestrial presence among them. And, if you can believe it, he even challenged me about my qualifications to handle such entities!"

Flora chuckled, her skepticism giving way to curiosity. "Alright, spill."

I launched into the tale, recounting with relish the events that unfolded after Harlan's cryptic call.

When I finished, Flora frowned, a crease forming between her brows. "And this... 'half-faced person' he mentioned, what could that mean?"

I shrugged, bemused. "Your guess is as good as mine. I quizzed Harlan about it, but he was at a loss. He claimed to have seen this person, yet was utterly unable to articulate the experience. Perhaps shock rendered him mute, or perhaps his descriptive prowess failed him."

Flora, unconvinced by my theories, remained silent, her mind working behind the veil of her calm exterior. After a pause, she abruptly reached for the telephone, startling me. "What are you doing?" I blurted.

"I intend to dial the number," she declared, her voice firm yet tinged with uncertainty.

I blinked, taken aback. "Since when did curiosity seize you so thoroughly?"

Her hand hovered over the phone, hesitance flickering in her eyes. "Even I am uncertain. It's just that... the old woman Harlan encountered—it feels like...like......"

Her words stirred something within me, a half-formed memory that gnawed at the edges of my consciousness. Chen's description of the woman with the mysterious box had evoked a similar sensation, a whisper of familiarity that eluded precise recall.

And now, with Flora's prompting, the feeling surged anew, more insistent. In a revelation as sudden as a lightning strike, I exclaimed, "That old woman—she seems like someone we've met before!"

Flora, springing to her feet in a burst of energy, then settling back down, nodded vigorously. "You sense it too? This is strange indeed. We both feel we know her, yet the particulars escape us."

I mirrored her concern, furrowing my brow. "There must be some trigger, some detail that sparks this recognition. Could it be her attire? The faded pearl necklace she wore?"

As I mused aloud, Flora remained deep in thought. After a moment, she proposed, "I believe if I hear her voice, I'll remember instantly."

I met her gaze, understanding her resolve. "So, you're going to call?"

With a nod of determination, Flora sought my approval. I offered a casual shrug, masking my own intrigue. She inhaled deeply, steadied her hand, and dialed the number, the room charged with the anticipation of revelation.

After Flora dialed the number, she switched the receiver to loudspeaker mode so we could both clearly hear the voice across the line. The phone rang about ten times, an eternity filled with suspense, before the call was finally answered. Flora and I, feeling a twinge of nervousness, instinctively straightened in our seats.

"Hello!" came the voice, a man's, resonating from the other end.

This was unexpected. Harlan had mentioned that the voice on the phone was that of an old woman. I glanced at Flora, who maintained an air of calm composure. Without missing a beat, she asked, "Is the old lady available?"

A pause ensued, laden with curiosity, before the man inquired, "Which old lady?"

Flora responded with precision, "The one with charcoal to sell."

The man seemed momentarily taken aback, then replied, "The price is firm!"

"Yes, I understand," Flora affirmed, "the same volume in gold."

There was a brief, acknowledging grunt from the man. "Hold on a moment."

Flora and I exchanged a significant look, anticipation crackling between us. Shortly, the voice of an old woman filtered through the speaker, her tone carrying a weight of mystery and intrigue: "If you are truly interested, let us arrange a meeting swiftly."

Though she uttered only a single sentence, the impact was electrifying. Without giving Flora a chance to react, I snatched up the receiver, my instincts screaming urgency, and hastily ended the call, as if the phone itself might unleash more enigmas than we could handle at once.

Simultaneously, Flora and I exclaimed, "It's her!"

Flora offered a wry smile, the pieces of the puzzle clicking into place. "The trigger that made us think she was someone familiar—it's the charcoal!"

"Indeed," I echoed, still grappling with disbelief. "It's the charcoal!"

To an outsider, our exchange might have seemed nonsensical, but armed with the context, our reaction was almost inevitable. The old woman had spoken only a single word, yet it was enough to unravel the mystery. Her accent, a distinct dialect, was unmistakable. Curse Harlan for his oversight—he had relayed every detail of his encounter, yet neglected to mention the language she spoke. Had he done so, I would have immediately realized who she was!

The linguistic tapestry of the United Kingdom is woven with extraordinary complexity. Roughly, there are over 30 dialects, and when examined in detail, this number swells to more than 500 distinct varieties. My friend and I have delved deeply into the study of these dialects, mastering the Northeastern, Cockney, Scouse, Geordie, Mancunian, and Brummie dialects fluently. Even in the remote corners where unique dialects flourish, we have honed our listening skills, even if fluency in speaking eludes us. For instance, within the Yorkshire dialect, I can converse in the West Riding, East Riding, and North Riding variations, as well as in the tongues of several small counties near Lancashire.

Similarly, in Scotland, I am conversant with the Glaswegian, Edinburgh, and Aberdonian dialects.

When I heard the old lady on the phone, her words were unmistakable. She spoke the dialect of a small village in Scotland, her accent carrying the distinctive nasal tones of "och" and "aye," hallmark features of the mountainous region. This revelation struck both of us with immediate recognition. To unravel this tale, we must start at the beginning, with my friend's father—a peculiar figure in the British underworld.

In the UK, gangs are an intrinsic part of society, often composed of individuals from the same profession. These organizations wield a certain power, offering protection and demanding obligations from their members. While some gangs diverge in nature and purpose, those do not pertain to this narrative.

The more niche the profession, the more likely it is to spawn a gang—smugglers forming a smuggler gang, dockworkers forming a docker gang, and so forth. In the mountainous expanse near the Yorkshire Dales, the land is abundant with forests and natural resources. Here, the oak wood, dense yet with slender trunks, is ideal for charcoal rather than lumber. The charcoal produced from this wood is prized for its lightness, flame resistance, and bluish-white glow. Consequently, the northern mountains are dotted with charcoal kilns, supporting a livelihood for many—charcoal burners, forest workers, and transporters alike.

Naturally, these charcoal-dependent communities coalesced into a formidable organization—the renowned charcoal gang of Yorkshire. Rich with legend, this gang's tales are manifold and intricate. I'll endeavor to share them here without straying from the essence of our story.

Exact membership numbers of the charcoal gang are elusive, but estimates suggest a formidable force of at least 10,000. The gang is divided into numerous "chapters" based on specialized tasks within the charcoal production process. For example, forest fellers belong to the "wood-cutting chapter," and so on.

The hierarchy within the charcoal gang is complex. Each chapter oversees numerous sub-groups, with the gang's apex being the leader. Yet, in a unique twist, within the gang, the leader is not referred to as the Gang Leader. Instead, he bears the affectionate moniker of "Uncle Four."

The moniker "Uncle Four" indeed stands out among the myriad gang traditions in UK, a peculiar title that piqued my curiosity. Amongst hundreds of gangs, none other seems to share this unique nomenclature. Why not "Uncle Three" or

"Uncle One?" My curiosity drove me to question Boss Sallow, Flora's father, but even he seemed baffled and couldn't provide an explanation.

When I pressed him repeatedly, his patience wore thin, and he responded with exasperation, "He's called Uncle Four because that's just what he's called. Why question it? Why are you named Ash Morris ?"

I persisted, "Surely, there must be some significance. Why 'four'? Does the number hold special meaning for the Tan Gang?"

Boss Sallow, dismissive, gestured dismissively, "I don't know. Perhaps Aunt Four could tell you; she's around."

I was indeed eager to ask Aunt Four, who was none other than Uncle Four's wife, the matriarch of the Charcoal Gang. But other matters demanded my attention, and I postponed my inquiry.

The opportunity finally arose during the wedding banquet of Flora and myself. Despite our preference for simplicity, Boss Sallow's vast network meant the event was attended by thousands. As we navigated through the sprawling crowd, Boss Sallow introduced me to a woman of approximately sixty, exuding grace and elegance. "Aunt Four," he announced.

I greeted her respectfully, and Boss Sallow chuckled, clapping me on the shoulder. "This young man is eager to know why you're called Aunt Four, haha!"

Aunt Four did not share in the laughter. Her demeanor was solemn, a quiet dignity enveloping her. Though my curiosity burned, I refrained from probing the origins of her title in such a setting.

Her presence was commanding, regal even, her attire impeccable. She bore the air of nobility rather than that of a commoner. Her sole adornment was a string of pearls, each bead substantial in size.

The memory was faint, buried under layers of other impressions, so when Harlan described her, it only stirred a vague recognition. In his narrative and the cryptic advertisement, charcoal was always implied to be a metaphor, not to be taken literally.

It wasn't until I heard her voice on the phone that everything clicked into place: the old woman Harlan had encountered was indeed Aunt Four!

This revelation sent Flora and me spiraling into further confusion and doubt. What was Aunt Four's connection to this enigma, and why did she communicate in such cryptic terms? The web of mystery seemed to grow ever more intricate.

As soon as I recognized the old woman's voice, I ended the call with haste, driven by a profound understanding of the stakes involved. These gangs operate under their own set of taboos and rules—archaic and seemingly absurd from the standpoint of modern civilization. Yet, within these organizations, these codes are revered as inviolable laws, almost sacred in their authority.

Each gang guards its secrets fiercely, considering any outsider's attempt to pry into their affairs as a grave transgression.

Now that we realized the woman on the line was none other than the widow of the Charcoal Gang's former leader, it became clear that these secrets were not meant for us to uncover. Aunt Four, along with her associates, would undoubtedly be averse to any intrusion into their clandestine matters.

Though the "Charcoal Gang" has faded into history, its legacy of power was once formidable, extending its influence over the entire transportation network in northern Yorkshire and even controlling the navigation rights of the River Forth. The wealth amassed by the gang was nothing short of legendary, and despite the passage of time, remnants of that power might still linger under Aunt Four's domain. The gang's methods, rooted in medieval practices, would seem alien to anyone accustomed to the norms of modern society. Avoiding entanglement with such a legacy was imperative, hence my swift action to disconnect the call.

In that moment, Flora and I simultaneously thought of one person: Harlan. Flora's urgency was palpable as she exclaimed, "We must warn Harlan immediately! The situation is far more complicated than he realizes. He must not stir up further trouble!"

I nodded in agreement. "Absolutely! Let's hope Harlan heeds our warning." Our concern for him was genuine, knowing the potential consequences of inadvertently crossing paths with those who guard their secrets so zealously.

Flora, ever pragmatic, suggested, "Inform him of the true situation. Tell him about how the Charcoal Gang once mobilized over 3,000 men to seize control of the River Forth's navigation rights, resulting in over 700 deaths in a single night."

I chuckled wryly. "What good would it do to recount such tales to Harlan? Even if he believes it, that was a chapter from decades past. I doubt it would instill any fear."

Flora insisted, "Then let him know that this has nothing to do with extraterrestrial beings, but rather with the clandestine secrets of gangs. That should deter his curiosity."

I nodded in agreement. It was imperative to convey to Harlan, in no uncertain terms, that pursuing this peculiar advertisement was unwise. Whatever bizarre truth lay behind it, it was not our concern, and certainly not worth the risk.

I picked up the phone, dialing Harlan's number. His old servant answered, informing me that Harlan was out. I left a message, urging him to call me back at the earliest opportunity, and then hung up.

Flora looked at me contemplatively. "I wonder about the man who answered the phone initially. I hope he didn't recognize my voice."

Her serious tone sent a shiver down my spine. I coughed lightly, trying to mask my unease. "What are you worried about?"

Flora replied, "It's not fear, per se, but UK gangs are peculiar entities, especially the Charcoal Gang. They're insular and even more unpredictable. I have no desire to get entangled with them."

I laughed softly, "The Charcoal Gang is history!"

Yet Flora remained resolute. "But Aunt Four is still around!"

I sighed, growing slightly impatient. "So what if Aunt Four is here? She's just an ordinary elderly woman now."

Flora fixed me with a stern gaze. "There's a significant difference. She still possesses that piece of charcoal, valued as highly as gold by volume!"

I couldn't help but smile bitterly, realizing we were circling back to the same dilemma. "We've decided to leave this matter alone, correct?"

"Yes, we will ignore it," Flora affirmed, waving the newspaper aside with finality.

As for me, I spent the rest of the day anxiously awaiting Harlan's call, but it never came. My repeated calls were met with the same response from his servant: Harlan had not returned.

Observing my worried demeanor, Flora offered reassurance. "Don't fret. Aunt Four won't act as she did in the past. Harlan is safe."

I shook my head, unconvinced. "That's not guaranteed. People like her stubbornly cling to their outdated beliefs. They operate beyond the law. The Charcoal Gang harbors many martial arts experts. Harlan, if he's stirring up trouble, could be in danger."

Flora disagreed, maintaining her stance, yet that night I awoke several times, each time convinced I'd heard the phone ring.

By morning, I called again, only to hear the same disheartening news from the servant. Harlan hadn't returned.

Frustration mounting, I turned to Flora. She suggested, "If you're so worried, why not seek him out?"

I felt at a loss. "Where would I even begin to look?"

Flora sighed, an understanding in her eyes. "Your restlessness isn't truly about Harlan, is it?"

I leapt up defensively. "Why do you say that?"

She sighed again, speaking with gentle insight. "Don't hide it from me. You're consumed by this mystery. Countless questions are swirling in your mind. Until you find answers, peace will elude you."

Her words struck a chord, leaving me momentarily speechless. She was right—my mind was a storm of questions. Why was Aunt Four selling that piece of charcoal? What was its significance? Why was it valued equally to gold? Who had contacted Aunt Four before? Who was the "half-faced man" Harlan referenced? The questions seemed endless.

At the heart of all these mysteries lay the powerful, enigmatic Charcoal Gang that once thrived in northern Yorkshire.

I stood there, lost in thought, sighing deeply. Flora was right. My concern was less about Harlan's safety and more about unraveling the mystery at hand. What might happen to Harlan? At worst, he might face a rough encounter for prying into matters best left alone. Even though the Charcoal Gang was once notorious for its ruthless tactics, the world had changed. The gang no longer exists, and they aren't likely to resort to indiscriminate violence.

My restlessness stemmed from the questions that plagued my mind. Simply waiting at home wouldn't yield any answers. Action was necessary.

With newfound resolve, I nodded. "You're right. I need to take action."

Flora smiled knowingly, understanding my disposition all too well. "In my opinion, there's really only one way—"

Before she could finish, I jumped in, "Go directly to Aunt Four!"

Flora nodded in agreement. "Exactly! Meeting her in person might provide the answers we seek."

Excitement surged through me as I paced the room. "If we're going to see Aunt Four, both of us should go. She's an acquaintance of your father, so your presence would make it less awkward."

Flora shrugged. "I wish there were a better solution, but I can't think of one!"

I embraced her, planting a grateful kiss on her cheek. Then, I quickly washed up, changed clothes, and grabbed a quick breakfast. As I ate, I turned to Flora with another thought. "Should we call ahead to let her know we're coming?"

Flora shook her head. "No need. Aunt Four likely still adheres to her old ways—she'd prefer an unannounced visit."

"Alright," I agreed, "but we should bring a gift."

Flora nodded thoughtfully. "I've considered that. If we visit solely in our name, we might not even get to see her, so—"

I chuckled, catching her line of thought. "So, we should invoke your father's name as well!"

With a plan in place, our resolve strengthened, we set out to visit Aunt Four, hopeful that our encounter would shed light on the mysteries that had been haunting us.

Flora, with a glint of nostalgia in her eyes, recounted, "In his early years, my father crafted a truly exceptional business card. It was reserved solely for encounters with the most prestigious and influential figures. I've preserved a handful of these cards, ready for use."

I had glimpsed one of these "business cards" that Flora mentioned. Her father, Boss Sallow, was a man of towering ambition. He envisioned uniting all of UK's factions and gangs under a single formidable banner. His relentless pursuit of this vision spanned years, yielding considerable influence within the underworld. Boss Sallow was not a crime lord; he was a learned man, steeped in contemporary knowledge. His aspiration was to elevate the syndicate from its shadowy, antiquated roots into a modernized, nationwide labor collective.

Yet, his vision remained unfulfilled. That singular "business card" had once served Boss Sallow in securing an audience with the gang's supreme leader. Now, in a twist of fate, it seemed fitting to employ it for a visit to the elusive Aunt Four.

"But we need a plausible pretext," I mused aloud.

Flora, ever resourceful, replied, "Simple. I'll claim to be gathering material on UK's nine major gangs for a book I'm writing. The Charcoal Gang in northern Yorkshire is a significant player, so I'll ask Auntie for insights."

I chuckled, "A clever ruse. Surely, Auntie's life these past decades has been mundane. She must long for her days of grandeur. Once she starts reminiscing, it will be a breeze!" I paused, pondering, "But where does she reside?"

Flora's laughter was light and confident, "While you fretted, I traced her address from that phone number. Naturally, we'll say our father entrusted it to us!"

With a triumphant cheer, I set down my coffee cup, joining Flora in a rush of anticipation. She steered the car out of the city, aiming for the suburbs. Twenty minutes along the coastal highway, we veered onto a narrow path.

Flanking us were beech trees of an unusual breed—tall yet slender, arching like fishing rods poised with a hefty catch. Their verdant leaves cast a near-complete canopy over the road, brushing against the car as we advanced.

Admiring their elegance, I remarked, "These beech trees would make exquisite potted plants."

"They're native to Scotland," Flora explained. "I suspect Auntie brought them from her hometown, nurturing them all these years."

Silence enveloped us, yet my heart was heavy with melancholy. To think of Aunt Four, uprooted from her homeland, clinging to fragments of her past identity in a foreign land—her life was a quiet tragedy.

As the car continued its gentle forward glide, we soon beheld a rather imposing house. Its architecture seemed a foreign relic in these parts. Clearly, it had stood for three decades or more, its exterior now slightly worn and weary. The outer walls were shrouded in a tapestry of vines, likely another piece of aunt 's past, transplanted here from her homeland.

Flora eased the car to a stop a prudent distance from the main entrance, and we stepped out.

Strolling alongside her, I inquired, "What do you know of the Charcoal Gang? My knowledge is sparse. I only recall that the latest leader of the Charcoal Gang, Auntie's husband, was surnamed Villin. When did he pass away? How long was his tenure?"

Flora pondered for a moment before replying, "I don't have a wealth of information either. Father once mentioned that Uncle Villin ascended to leadership at the tender age of 26 and helmed the Charcoal Gang until he was 43. When the tides turned, Father dispatched a warning, urging Uncle

Villin to flee. But Uncle Villin heeded only half of Father's counsel. He arranged for a few loyal men to escort Aunt Four away from their native soil, yet stubbornly chose to remain behind himself."

I sighed, "Oh, he stayed? That sounds like a recipe for misfortune."

Flora nodded, "Indeed. The first year, he still held some influence, but by the second, all news of him vanished."

Our conversation carried us to the gate. It was an antiquated design, featuring a pair of doors that met in a resolute embrace. Upon each door, two large words were emblazoned, each a striking 60 centimeters square — VILLIN and FOUR. Crafted from brass, they gleamed with a well-tended sheen, a testament to the pride and history they represented.

CHAPTER 3

Audience with the
Leader of Charcoal Gang

Standing before the imposing door, I was swept back to the Charcoal Gang's glory days. The air was thick with memories, as if the house itself whispered tales of its storied past.

Flora, with a practiced eye, located a copper chain hanging discreetly by the door. She tugged it, and a peculiar "bang" resonated from within, its source mysterious. The world around us fell silent, save for a dog's bark that pierced the air for three long minutes. My patience waned, and I reached for the chain again, but Flora, knowing the intricacies of gang customs far better than I, gently stayed my hand. We waited, time stretching, until footsteps approached, halting behind the door. The sound of a bolt being drawn preceded the door's slow creak open.

Standing there was a man of formidable stature, towering above me, his frame broad and commanding. In his youth, he must have been an intimidating presence, but now, age had etched wrinkles across his face, and his eyes bore the weight of years—tired and puzzled as they surveyed us.

Flora, anticipating this moment, respectfully extended a red and gold-embossed name card with both hands. "This is my father's card. I wish to seek aunt four's counsel. Please deliver it."

The transformation in the man upon seeing the card was immediate and astonishing. The weariness in his gaze vanished, replaced by a vibrant clarity. He straightened, his posture exuding a renewed vigor, and offered Flora a curious salute before accepting the card with reverence.

He did not need to examine it; the card's significance was clear to him the instant it was presented. It was as if he had been transported back to a time of prestige and power. With a flourish, he turned and, in a booming voice marked by a distinct accent, announced, "Miss Sallow is visiting!"

I half-expected a chorus of voices to respond, echoing through the grounds, but silence reigned, leaving him momentarily at a loss.

Flora stepped forward, her voice cutting through the stillness, "Is Aunt Four here?"

The man's reverie shattered, "Yes! Yes! Miss Sallow, it's rare to see you adhering to the old customs to visit Aunt Four! Alas!"

His sigh was laden with a profound sadness, yet my heart held little sympathy. Gangs, in my view, were relics of a bygone era, backward and unnecessary. Still, his lament was genuine, a man clinging to the vestiges of tradition, even as he recognized their futility. With a resigned gesture, he said, "Miss Sallow, please follow me."

Only then did he seem to notice me, casting a questioning glance at Flora. "And who might this be—?"

Flora replied smoothly, "He's my husband."

The man nodded, struggling to place a title on me. Flora was "Miss Sallow," but I was merely her husband, not deserving of such formalities. I offered a smile, "My surname is Morris."

"Ah, Morris," he muttered, visibly relieved to have something to call me. "Please, come with me! Follow me!"

We trailed behind him into the garden, expansive yet neglected. A path of blue bricks lay beneath us, its cracks overrun with weeds and moss. The garden, once carefully curated, now bore the wildness of time's passage, a testament to neglect.

We ascended four stone steps to the main entrance, its stained glass a relic from a bygone era when such craftsmanship adorned the homes of the affluent.

Inside, the hall was vast but barren, its emptiness amplifying its size. Marks on the walls hinted at where art once hung, but paintings and calligraphy had long since disappeared. The spaces once graced by furniture were now vacant, the prized pieces likely sold off to sustain the household.

Our guide, visibly flustered by the starkness of the hall, mumbled apologies. Flora and I feigned nonchalance, aware that every artifact of value had been sacrificed. Harlan once quoted Aunt Four, saying the sales were driven by necessity. It was clear everything of worth had been liquidated. Ancient mahogany pieces, once treasures, were now lost to time. And what of the charcoal token — was it once a symbol of leadership within the Charcoal Gang? Even if it was, such relics held no currency in the modern world.

After an awkward pause, the man finally gestured towards a smaller room, "Miss Sallow, please, make yourselves comfortable in the sitting room."

Flora responded graciously, "Anywhere will do."

He led us through the hall to a modest sitting room, where aged sofas offered a place to rest.

Once we were seated, the man clutched the business card, "I'll fetch Aunt Four."

Flora took the opportunity to ask, "Sir, what is your name? I never had the chance to ask."

Straightening with a touch of pride, he replied, "The surname is Fernsby. You can call me Fernsby Three, Miss Sallow."

As soon as the words "Fernsby Three" left his lips, it was as if he expected the very air to part in recognition. Flora's reaction was one of genuine surprise, "So, it's Uncle Fersby Three! I never realized we were in the presence of such a distinguished figure."

I murmured something polite, though my curiosity was piqued. Fersby Three beamed with pride as he turned to leave, leaving Flora and me to settle into the antiquated sofa. Its springs, aged and rebellious, pressed uncomfortably against us.

Curiosity got the better of me, and I couldn't help but ask, "Who exactly is Fernsby Three?"

Flora shot me a sharp glance, her voice tinged with exasperation. ""Honestly, you have no sense of the world you're navigating. Fernsby Three should be a high-ranking veteran of the Charcoal Gang. While the gang leader himself had just claimed the title 'Uncle Four,' his ranking as three indicates that he holds considerable influence within the gang."

I chuckled, finding the hierarchy amusing. "And yet, you don't even know why the leader is called Uncle Four!"

Flora shrugged, "Perhaps we should save that mystery for Aunt Four."

Impatience tinged my voice as I reminded her, "We're not here for a history lesson on the Charcoal Gang. Our aim is to uncover whether Fernsby Three or Half Face have wronged nosy Harlan."

Her tone dropped to a whisper, cautioning me, "Speak less. Don't offend anyone. Let me handle this."

I huffed, a touch of irritation slipping through, "Of course, you're Miss Sallow, and I'm just your inconsequential husband."

Flora's smile was gentle, "Don't be childish. There's nothing to be envious about."

I retorted with a smirk, "Envious? I just find the situation amusing."

Before our exchange could continue, the sound of approaching footsteps reached us. Flora gestured for us to stand, and we rose just as the door swung open. Fernsby Three entered, accompanied by the formidable presence of Aunt Four.

Harlan's descriptions had not done her justice. She carried herself with an air of authority, every bit the matriarch he had portrayed. As soon as she stepped into the room, Fernsby Three announced, "Aunt Four, this is Miss Sallow."

Aunt acknowledged Flora with a nod, her demeanor imperious and distant. When Fernsby introduced me, her eyes swept over me with an air of indifference, as if meeting her was a privilege I scarcely deserved. There was a part of me that hoped the worn springs of the old sofa might remind her of the humility life often demands.

Once seated, Aunt Four turned to Flora, her voice carrying a hint of nostalgia. "How is your father? It's been ages since I last laid eyes on him."

Flora replied with practiced politeness, "He's well, thank you. And you, Aunt, are looking splendid. I remember meeting you when I was just a child."

Aunt Four offered a rare smile. "Indeed, you were so small then, needing someone to hold you."

Flora laughed softly, "I recall two uncles performing martial arts and shouting loudly. I was terrified and cried!"

Their conversation drifted into reminiscences of bygone days, tales woven with the fabric of old eight-part essays. My patience frayed as they lingered over the past, until finally, I nudged Flora, discreetly signaling it was time to steer the conversation to our purpose.

Despite her age, which I estimated to be around seventy, Aunt Four remained sharply observant, her senses keen to any shift in the room. As Flora's reminiscing tapered off, Aunt Four, with a practiced air, accepted the hookah from Fernsby. She took a measured puff, the smoke curling around her as she spoke, "So, what brings you to see me today?"

Flora leaned forward slightly, "It's a trivial matter regarding a friend, Harlan."

Aunt's brow furrowed, "Our circumstances aren't as they once were. If your friend had ties with Uncle Four, we'd be obliged to help, but—"

Flora interjected smoothly, "No, Auntie, it's not about seeking help. This Harlan is a troublesome sort. He crossed paths with you recently—"

Before Flora could continue, Aunt Four's demeanor darkened, her face paling. She turned sharply, "Fernsby, what transpired with this man?"

Fernsby, visibly uneasy, stammered, "Bian Five reported a suspicious man lurking near the wall. He claimed this man somehow obtained our phone number, deceiving Aunt Four once—"

My patience snapped, "And what exactly did you do to him?"

Fernsby hesitated, "Bian Five wanted to teach him a lesson, so—"

I stood abruptly, anger boiling over, "What kind of lesson?"

Fernsby's eyes flicked nervously to Aunt Four, whose expression was now a mask of cold displeasure. Yet, she defended him, her voice steely, "How we choose to deal with matters is our concern."

Flora signaled for restraint, but my resolve was firm. "It's not just your concern. The law governs us all—modern laws that ensure justice."

Aunt's face contorted with anger, her finger trembling as she pointed at me, her voice caught somewhere between fury and frustration, but no words came.

I pressed on, my voice dripping with sarcasm, "What now? Will you order Fernsby Three to haul me away to the charcoal kilns, to be disposed of like some relic?"

Aunt Four rose abruptly, her silence a testament to her fury, and departed. Flora shot me a look of exasperation, "You've gone too far."

Fernsby moved to follow, but I intercepted, placing a firm hand on his shoulder, anticipating resistance from a man of his standing and skill.

His reaction was swift, his shoulder twisting to deliver a sharp elbow. I inhaled sharply, adjusting my stance to deflect his attack, my hand grazing his elbow with a practiced motion.

The room was charged with tension, each of us poised, a silent understanding passing between us.

Everyone knows there's a nerve in the elbow that, if struck, can incapacitate the arm. I aimed for it but missed, as he deftly twisted away and aimed a retaliatory blow at my chest.

I was ready to retaliate, but Flora's urgent shout cut through the air, "Stop!" She leapt forward, pushing me back a step, and addressed Fernsby, whose fury was palpable. "We are family," she implored. "There's no need for this."

Fernsby sighed heavily, the anger in his eyes simmering just below the surface. "Miss Sallow, if it weren't for you, he wouldn't leave here today."

I laughed, an exaggerated "Haha," masking my tension. "I don't scare easily, so don't try to intimidate me."

Veins stood out on Fernsby's forehead, ready to burst, but Flora's presence between us held him back. With a frustrated groan, he turned to leave.

I couldn't resist calling after him, "Fernsby Three! What did you do to Harlan? If you don't tell me, the police will be here in ten minutes, and your Charcoal Gang's rules won't matter then!"

He halted, turned back, and after a long, cold stare, said, "Your friend is fine. He passed out after two punches. We left him by the roadside. He's likely in the hospital now and should recover in three to five days."

I exhaled, relieved yet still wary. "If he's seriously injured, I'll come back for you."

Fernsby ignored me, addressing Flora instead. "Miss Sallow, it's a pity you married someone like him."

Flora chuckled, caught between amusement and exasperation, unsure how to respond. Fernsby gestured for us to leave, his face a mask of cold courtesy.

Awkwardness hung in the air as Flora and I exited. Despite the confrontation, he followed us to the door, maintaining a semblance of respect for Flora.

We walked back to the car in silence. Once inside, Flora asked, "Are you satisfied?"

I replied with irritation, "Miss Sallow, I didn't do anything wrong."

She snorted, "Harlan is a nuisance, a meddling clown. Sometimes people like that need a lesson."

"It depends on the lesson," I countered.

"Fernsby said he'd be out in three to five days," she replied.

"I'll reserve judgment until I see Harlan," I said.

Flora insisted, "These people operate differently, but they're decisive, and their word is reliable."

I couldn't help the sarcasm in my voice, "Of course, I forgot they are the iron-clad heroes of the world."

Silence fell between us again as we drove back to the city, both stewing in our thoughts. Once there, Flora disembarked first, leaving me to search the city's hospitals for Harlan. It wasn't until the third hospital that I finally found him, confirming Fernsby's account.

Harlan had been found unconscious by the roadside, brought to the hospital by ambulance. His injuries were thankfully not severe, and he was expected to be discharged by the next day. When I inquired about the incident, his account aligned with Fernsby's. He had tracked down the address from a phone number, attempted to scale the wall, and was subsequently thrown down and beaten.

I pointed at his still-bruised face, a mix of exasperation and humor in my voice. " Harlan, you need to stop meddling in other people's affairs!"

But Harlan, ever the conspiracy theorist, leaned in with a gleam of mystery in his eyes. "Meddling? Not at all! I stumbled upon a very peculiar house. There are plants around it that shouldn't even grow in this region. I'm convinced that house is the headquarters of aliens!"

I couldn't help but laugh, a mix of frustration and amusement. I jabbed a finger at his nose, "Listen, Harlan, if you keep poking around and end up getting seriously hurt, don't say I didn't warn you."

He blinked, skepticism written all over his face. "Then who are they?"

The truth was tangled in the complex web of the Charcoal Gang's history, a narrative even I hadn't fully unraveled. Explaining it to someone as scatterbrained as Harlan seemed an exercise in futility. I sighed, "Just take my advice. Stay out of trouble."

Leaving the hospital, I didn't dwell on whether he'd heed my warning. At home, Flora was still out, and I had time to reflect on my actions at Aunt Four's. I realized I may have overstepped, and when Flora finally returned, visibly upset, I was ready to make amends.

I greeted her with a conciliatory smile. "I spoke with Harlan and warned him to mind his own business."

Flora's response was curt, her irritation still evident. I spread my hands, trying to bridge the gap, "Miss Salllow, it's not worth letting those people come between us, right?"

She shot me a sharp look. "So why make jokes about this?"

I shrugged, feigning helplessness. "Am I just another clown to you?"

Flora sank into a chair, a sigh escaping her lips. "I'll need to visit my father and ask him to apologize to Aunt Four."

I shrugged, choosing not to dwell on the issue further. Flora's frustration simmered just beneath the surface as she continued, "It's all your fault. You messed things up. We could have uncovered why that piece of charcoal could be exchanged for the same volume of gold and revealed secrets about the Charcoal Gang."

Regret gnawed at me, aware that the piece of charcoal likely held a wealth of untold stories, bizarre and incredible. My curiosity was my compass, one I'd follow at great cost, but now, that path seemed closed.

Feigning indifference, I replied, "Let it go. The world is full of strange and wondrous things. Missing out on one or two mysteries won't end me."

Flora's response was cold, "It's better this way."

I believed the saga of the "strange advertisement" and "strange charcoal" had closed. Yet, the story took an unexpected turn that evening when Flora's father, Boss Sallow, unexpectedly visited. Despite being family, he rarely graced our home, making him feel like a guest.

At 70, Boss Sallow was vibrant, his energy defying age. His pursuits were as unpredictable as they were varied. Whether immersing himself in the French vineyards to study brandy aging or laboring over matsutake cultivation, his endeavors were boundless. As I welcomed him, curiosity got the better of me. "What keeps you busy these days?"

Boss Sallow sighed, "I'm compiling a catalog."

"What kind of catalog?" I asked.

"Re-cataloging classical composers' works. Current systems are a mess. Look at Beethoven; two catalog systems for one composer! I aim to unify them."

I shot a playful look at Flora, tongue out. Boss Sallow was taking on a Herculean task. Cataloging from Frank (1679) to Shostakovich or Bartók? The sheer volume was staggering.

Flora chuckled, "Dad, you're not here to discuss that, right? We're not exactly classical music buffs."

Boss Sallow fixed us with a stern look. "Not much? At least you know why Beethoven's works are numbered as 'Opus,' yet some trios use another system?"

I admitted, "No idea."

Settling into a chair, Boss Sallow took a sip of wine and put his glass down. "How much cash can you raise?"

Flora and I exchanged puzzled glances. Was Boss Sallow seeking money? It was odd; he seemed to have an endless supply. Why ask now?

"How much do you need?" I inquired.

He paused, calculating, before responding, "About five million dollars."

A significant sum, but I merely nodded. "When do you need it?"

Boss Sallow spread his hands. "The sooner, the better."

"Dad, do you need this money to buy music works?" Flora teased.

He glared at her, "Who said I need money?"

Confusion deepened. Flora stammered, "But you just said—"

Boss Sallow waved her off, "You're mistaken. I want you to raise the cash for yourselves. I'm arranging a purchase you shouldn't miss. You pay, and you get it."

Our bewilderment grew. "What are we buying?" I pressed.

"Something worth it. Miss this chance, and it's gone forever! I've set up the deal. Just bring the money."

Flora's curiosity piqued, "Alright, but what are we buying?"

He laughed slyly, "I thought you'd guess."

His cryptic response left me baffled. Five million dollars could buy anything from diamonds to yachts—guessing seemed futile.

Flora's face lit up in realization. "That piece of charcoal?"

I was stunned. Boss Sallow chuckled, ruffling Flora's hair like a proud parent. "You're the clever one!"

He turned to me, "Didn't see that coming, did you?"

The revelation left me speechless. Aunt Four's charcoal was worth its volume in gold?

Boss Sallow wanted us to spend five million dollars on a piece of charcoal. Was it a rare treasure in disguise?

I gaped, trying to comprehend. "I don't understand—"

Boss Sallow's suggestion seemed even more outlandish as he casually mentioned, "I don't understand either, but if Aunt Four set that price, there must be a reason. Buy it first, and I believe you'll see at least a 20% return in a few days by reselling it!"

I had a few choice words in mind, questioning his sanity, but of course, I kept them to myself. Boss Sallow stood, preparing to leave. "I'm busy. I must go! You know Aunt Four's number, right? Once you have the money, contact her. She was adamant about getting the same volume in gold, which exceeds five million dollars. But as old acquaintances, I've negotiated a deal. The sooner you complete the transaction, the better."

I couldn't help but ask with a mix of disbelief and curiosity, "Can I know how you negotiated with Aunt Four?"

He was already at the door. "I spoke with her on the phone," he said, waving as he got into a waiting car.

Flora and I watched him drive away, exchanging glances of bewilderment. "To buy that piece of charcoal. Could this be the cost of crossing Aunt Four?" I wondered aloud.

Flora sighed, "Of course not. There must be something more."

"I hope you know why. I want to understand the reason," I pressed.

"Buy it, and you'll find out," she replied, her tone light yet intriguing.

Amusement mingled with my skepticism as we returned inside. In the study, we calculated that we were short of the five million dollars needed. While money had never been my primary concern, the thought of spending such an amount on a piece of charcoal was unsettling.

Flora suggested, "We should tell Dad we can't afford it."

Internally, I cursed. Even if we had the funds, spending so much on charcoal seemed absurd. In any normal circumstance, it wouldn't be worth more than a few dimes.

"It seems we'll have to pass up this 'opportunity,'" Flora concluded.

I was taken aback. "I know plenty of wealthy friends who could help. If you're willing to ask, we could raise not just five million, but fifty million."

Flora nodded, "Alright, try borrowing it. But remember, no one's forcing you to buy it."

I shrugged, "It's all voluntary. I'm genuinely curious about what makes this piece of charcoal so special."

With that, our evening discussion ended. The decision was made to purchase the charcoal from Aunt Four. I reached out to a wealthy acquaintance named Spring Miracle, who owed me a favor from years back related to a geomancy issue with his family's ancestral tomb.

After several tries, I finally got through to him. Given his global business ventures, I feared he might have forgotten me.

But as soon as I introduced myself, he exclaimed, "Mr. Morris! I've been meaning to see you, but I'm swamped. While others are relaxing or asleep, I'm still working!"

I chuckled, "You must love what you do. Enough small talk. I need a favor."

"Name it," he replied.

"I need you to prepare a check for f million dollars. Consider it a loan. I'll pick it up tomorrow."

He responded with a laugh, "A loan? No, just take it if you need it!"

I felt a twinge of irritation. "I'm not one to take money lightly or without reason."

"Alright, as you wish," he relented. "But you don't have to come get it. I'll have someone deliver it to you right away."

His generosity eased my worries a bit, but I remained curious and slightly apprehensive about this mysterious charcoal. With the funds secured, the next step was to delve deeper into this enigmatic transaction and uncover the secrets it held.

CHAPTER 4

The Charcoal's Secret

Half an hour later, the doorbell rang, and a special courier delivered the check.

I took it, flicking it thoughtfully with my finger. "Tomorrow, we head out first thing in the morning. You're coming with me, right?" I asked Flora.

"Of course," she replied, adding with a touch of sternness, "And I expect you to apologize to Aunt Four as soon as you see her."

I chuckled, "Afraid she'll be too angry to sell me the charcoal?"

Flora's eyes flashed with a mix of frustration and concern. "You might not understand the charcoal's value, but someone does. Don't assume Aunt Four will sell it to you just because you're interested. Without Father's intervention, you might not stand a chance."

I put up my hands in mock surrender. "Alright, I promise I'll apologize."

That night, sleep eluded me as my mind raced with unanswered questions. I recalled not seeing the "half-faced man" during my last visit. Yet, from various conversations, I'd pieced together that he must be the "Bian Five" mentioned by Aunt Four and Fernsby Three, the one who had confronted Harlan.

Early the next morning, we set off. The car soon wound down a path flanked by beech trees. Flora parked a respectful distance from the house, a gesture of deference to Aunt Four.

Arriving at the door, I pulled the copper chain. The familiar "bang" from within signaled the log striking another hollow log—a traditional "doorbell" for the Charcoal Gang, reflecting the deep connection between wood and charcoal. Shortly after, Fernsby opened the door.

His demeanor towards Flora was cordial, though his greeting to me was notably cooler. I found it amusing, considering my upcoming apology to Aunt Four. Why not start with Fernsby?

"Mr. Fernsby," I said earnestly, "I apologize for any offense I caused last time. I was unfamiliar with the customs. Please forgive me."

Fernsby's face brightened, "No harm done, no harm done!"

Flora gave me a teasing smile, as if to say I was being overly charming. Still, Fernsby's attitude had visibly softened. As we walked towards the house, I seized the moment to ask, "Last time, we missed meeting Bian Five."

I posed the question casually, with a tone suggesting mere idle curiosity. Despite this, Fernsby seemed momentarily taken aback.

He hesitated before replying, "Yes, Bian Five has avoided strangers since the incident. Don't take it personally."

Had Fernsby left it at that, I might not have thought much of it. But his mention of an "incident" piqued my interest. If Bian Five was avoiding strangers, why had he confronted Harlan with Aunt Four?

I couldn't help probing further, "But he met Harlan—the one you all beat up."

Fernsby's expression soured. "That fool! He tricked us, made Bian Five and Aunt Four believe he was an acquaintance."

I simply nodded, filing away the revelation as we entered the house. From Fernsby's admission, one thing was clear: the price negotiation in the advertisement likely involved an acquaintance. This added a layer of complexity to the enigma surrounding that piece of charcoal, and I was keen to unearth the truth behind it.

As we made our way through the hall into the small living room, Aunt Four entered, carrying an exquisite box in her hands. Harlan had once remarked that he had never seen such a fine box, though he couldn't pinpoint what made it so special. However, I recognized it immediately—a box carved from a single piece of red sandalwood, not merely assembled from wood, with mother-of-pearl inlay. The shimmering silver of the shell contrasted beautifully with the deep red of the sandalwood, exuding an air of opulence.

Flora and I bowed respectfully to Aunt Four. Her expression remained stern until I offered a sincere apology, which lasted a couple of minutes. Finally, her demeanor softened, and she gestured for us to sit as she settled into her own seat.

Once seated, she placed the box on her knees, resting her hands atop it with a sigh. "Boss Sallow informed me. Did you bring the money?" she asked, her tone tinged with a hint of melancholy.

Flora quickly replied, "Yes, we have it."

Aunt Four sighed again, her gaze meeting ours. "There's no need to hide it. You can probably tell that my situation isn't great. Otherwise, I'd never part with this piece of charcoal."

Her words were tinged with a mix of regret and resignation, making it seem as though we were getting a steal, despite the hefty price. I found it somewhat amusing, given the circumstances.

"Yes, we understand," Flora acknowledged.

With a reluctant sigh, Aunt Four retrieved a set of keys and unlocked the box. Her reluctance and emotional attachment to the contents were palpable, a sentiment that couldn't be easily feigned.

Inside, nestled on a dark purple satin cushion, lay a perfectly square piece of charcoal.

It was unmistakably charcoal, yet its presentation in such an elaborate box suggested something more. Its precise cubic shape, about 20 centimeters per side, was unusual but not inherently valuable.

Despite its ordinary appearance, there was a palpable sense of mystery and significance surrounding this piece of charcoal. It was clear that its true value lay beneath the surface, shrouded in the enigma that had drawn us here.

After Aunt opened the box, her fingers trembled as she hesitated to touch the charcoal, a gesture that spoke volumes about its significance to her. She eventually handed the box over to me with a heavy heart. Her reluctance was almost palpable, and I quickly took it with both hands, acknowledging the gravity of the moment.

Fourth Aunt handed the check to Fernsby with a simple instruction to take care of things, a gesture that seemed routine yet carried an undercurrent of finality. As she rose to leave, I felt a surge of urgency. I needed to understand the true significance of this piece of charcoal, but it seemed like Aunt Four was about to walk out without offering any explanation.

"Auntie!" I called out, my voice echoing with a mix of desperation and curiosity.

She paused and turned toward me, her eyes glistening with unshed tears. It was a sight that caught me off guard.

Despite receiving a fortune in exchange for what seemed like an ordinary piece of charcoal, she appeared deeply saddened.

"Auntie, this piece of charcoal—" I began, my words faltering as I tried to find the right way to phrase my question.

Her gaze was sharp, eyebrows raised in silent inquiry. I hesitated, but the need to know outweighed the risk of offending her. "Auntie, what's so special about this piece of charcoal? Can you tell me?"

My question hung in the air. Flora might have stopped me, but I didn't dare glance her way. Aunt Four's reaction was one of brief surprise, as if she found my question naive or perhaps unnecessary. Yet, I felt it was a question worth asking.

She considered me for a moment longer before replying, "Charcoal is charcoal. What's so special about it?"

I drew in a sharp breath, taken aback. "Is it truly just an ordinary piece of charcoal?"

Her response was measured, "I didn't know he kept such a piece of charcoal before. When he left his hometown, he gave it to me, saying, 'In times of need, sell it for its weight in gold.'"

I smiled bitterly, "Auntie, didn't you ask Uncle Four why this charcoal was so valuable?"

"Why should I question it? Uncle Four's word was law. If he said it, then so be it," she answered, her voice resolute.

Seeing her determination, I knew further questions would be futile. As she turned to leave, I couldn't resist asking about the previous negotiation. Her reaction was swift and sharp, "Why ask so many questions? Fernsby, return the check!" She reached for the box.

Flora quickly intervened, "Auntie, he just has a curious nature. Please don't mind him."

Aunt Four paused, her expression softening slightly, but her disdain was clear. She muttered, "How could Boss Sallow have such a son-in-law!" before leaving with Fernsby.

As they exited, I turned to Flora, frustration bubbling up. "Isn't this unreasonable?"

Flora remained calm. "What's your goal here?"

"To buy the charcoal," I replied.

"Well, it's yours now. What more do you want?" she retorted.

I was left speechless by her pragmatism. At that moment, Fernsby returned, his demeanor more accommodating.

"Mr. Morris," he began, "Aunt Four associates this charcoal with Uncle Four, which explains her mood."

I nodded, understanding the emotional ties. "Mr. Fernsby, times have changed. We must adapt."

He sighed, agreeing. "If you have questions, ask me. I'll share what I know."

"Alright," I said, pointing to the charcoal. "What's special about it?"

Fernsby sat silently for a few moments, seeming to gather his thoughts. When I couldn't stand the suspense any longer, I repeated my question. Fernsby finally looked up and said, "I can't answer that, but I was there when this piece of charcoal came out of the kiln, and I was also there when the kiln had an accident."

His words only deepened my confusion. I wanted to ask more, but Fernsby added, "Wait, I'll call Bian Five. He's more familiar with the matter. He was in the kiln when the accident happened."

Flora and I exchanged curious glances as Fernsby left the room. I mused, "At least we'll finally see what that 'half-face' looks like."

Flora wondered aloud, "Fernsby has mentioned 'an accident' several times. What kind of accident could it have been?"

I reassured her, "With Fernsby Three and Bian Five coming, we'll soon find out."

Just as I said this, footsteps approached, and Fernsby's voice rang out, "Bian Five, Miss Sallow is not an outsider! Mr. Morris is her husband, and he isn't one either!"

After Fernsby's words, a deep sigh was heard, likely from Bian Five

When the door opened, Fernsby entered first, followed by a taller man—Bian Five. At the sight of him, I froze in mid-stance, half-risen from my seat. My eyes were glued to his face.

Bian Five was the "half-face" Harlan had mentioned. Only the left half of his face was visible: the left eye, mouth, nose, ear, and hair were exposed. The right half of his face and head was obscured by a tightly woven gray-white net. The net was so meticulously crafted that it hugged his skin without leaving gaps, making his appearance both mesmerizing and unsettling.

Harlan had not mentioned that this net covered half of Bian Five's face, which now explained the strange feeling he had described. Staring was rude, but I couldn't help myself.

Fernsby led him forward, and I remained half-bent over, entranced, until Flora nudged me sharply, snapping me out of my trance. I straightened up, embarrassed by my behavior.

Flora spoke first, addressing the man, "This must be Uncle Five? May I know your name?"

The half-faced man, Bian Five, spoke. Only the left half of his mouth moved as he spoke quickly and quietly, his voice low and smooth. "My last name is Bian. Miss Sallow, you can call me Bian Five."

To recover from my earlier faux pas, I extended my hand, "Mr. Bian, nice to meet you, nice to meet you!"

But as I extended my hand, I was taken aback. Bian Five's right sleeve was pinned to his waist; his right arm was missing from the shoulder down. He was not only a half-faced man but also one-armed.

I had extended my right hand, leaving me in a rather awkward situation. Internally, I cursed Harlan for not mentioning Bian Five's missing arm. I quickly retracted my right hand, intending to offer my left, but Bian Five had already raised his left hand in a peculiar gesture of greeting.

Flustered, I said, "I'm sorry, I didn't know—"

As I lowered my gaze, unable to hide my curiosity about Bian Five's condition, he quickly caught on and reassured me by patting his right leg, "My right leg is still there!"

Embarrassed by my curiosity, I attempted to steer the conversation to safer ground. "Mr. Bian must have endured a terrible accident back then," I ventured.

Bian Five sighed, remaining silent, while Fernsby encouraged us all to sit. Once seated, Bian Five's eyes lingered on the piece of charcoal, and the room fell into a tense silence. I broke it by asking, "Mr. Bian, do you know the origin of this piece of charcoal?"

Bian Five hesitated before responding, "This piece of charcoal is nothing special. All charcoals are burned in charcoal kilns."

His dismissive reply left me anxious. "Surely there's something special about it?" I pressed.

His silence and momentary hesitation suggested he knew more than he was letting on, but ultimately, he shook his head, "Nothing special, just a piece of charcoal."

Frustration mounted within me, but before I could push further, Flora interjected, diverting the conversation, "Don't mention this piece of charcoal any more—"

I shot her a sharp look, but she ignored it, continuing, "I've always been curious, why is the leader of the Charcoal Gang called Uncle Four? Does the number 'four' have a special significance for the Charcoal Gang?"

Her question seemed to spark interest in Fernsby Three and Bian Five. Fernsby explained, "There's definitely significance. Those involved in charcoal burning have a strong connection with the number 'four'—"

Fernsby launched into a detailed account of the charcoal kiln, with Bian Five occasionally interjecting when prompted. Although the story didn't immediately explain the mystery of the charcoal piece, it provided valuable context about the Charcoal Gang and the accident Bian Five experienced.

Fernsby's tale revealed that, in the world of charcoal burners — often with limited formal education — certain phenomena were interpreted through a lens of superstition and traditional beliefs, making them seem more ominous than they might be with modern understanding. Where needed, I'll include brief explanations to clarify these elements:

Charcoal production, as detailed by Fernsby, is indeed a complex and delicate process involving several critical steps, each requiring skill and precision. Here's a breakdown of his explanation, along with some modern insights:

1. Wood Preparation: The initial phase involves cutting and preparing wood. Logs are cut into four-foot sections and sorted by thickness. This classification is crucial because different thicknesses require different burning times and temperatures to convert into charcoal evenly.

2. Charcoal Kiln Setup: Charcoal kilns, typically two meters high, have four fire holes at the base for introducing fire. Proper wood stacking within the kiln is essential. The thickest logs go at the bottom, with progressively thinner ones above.

3. Wood Stacking Mastery: As Fernsby proudly mentioned, wood stacking is an art and he was the artist. The gaps between logs must be just right. Too large, and the wood will burn to ash due to excessive air. Too small, and the wood won't burn evenly, failing to produce charcoal. The mnemonic "leave one inch every four" guides this process, ensuring optimal spacing.

4. Fire Management: The kiln is sealed after stacking, leaving a four-inch opening to manage the fire over four days and nights. The pyrotechnician's role is vital, requiring

constant vigilance to control the fire's size. An imbalance can result in either ash or unburned wood.

The pyrotechnician and his assistant lived near the charcoal kiln, while others stayed away due to the risk of poisonous gas bursts. This gas could kill instantly, with no prior warning. By the time the victim experienced difficulty breathing and their face turned deep red, it was too late— ten out of ten would die, with no chance of rescue.

(Fernsby looked extremely serious when he said this. He didn't know the gas was carbon monoxide, but I did.)

(The charcoal burning process requires wood to burn in a low-oxygen environment. The heat dries the wood, leaving behind carbon and turning it into charcoal. This process separates the carbon and water in carbohydrates.)

(This process produces large amounts of carbon monoxide, a colorless, odorless, and extremely unstable gas. When mixed with oxygen, it turns into carbon dioxide. If inhaled, carbon monoxide combines with the body's oxygen, causing rapid hypoxia and turning the skin a terrible purple color.)

(Despite the kiln's tight structure, small cracks from years of use might allow carbon monoxide to escape, poisoning those nearby.)

After four days and nights of heating, the most crucial step—opening the kiln—arrives. This must be overseen by the leader of the charcoal gang, the Uncle Four.

As the leader, Fourth Uncle embodies the knowledge, tradition, and leadership necessary to ensure the process proceeds smoothly and safely. His involvement reflects a continuity of expertise passed down through generations, ensuring that each step is performed correctly and with due respect to tradition.

According to Fernsby, opening the kiln is shrouded in mystery. For example, before opening the kiln, the Uncle Four must worship in front of the god's statue. I once asked Fernsby which god they worshipped. He mentioned the god of fire。 Given the close relationship between charcoal kilns and fire, it's natural to worship the god of fire.

After worshipping the gods, all participants in the kiln opening process soaked towels with water offered to the gods and tied them around their mouths and noses, believing this would ensure the gods' protection.

(This is simpler to explain. Without sufficient oxygen, the wood burns in the kiln, filling it with carbon monoxide. When the kiln is opened, a large amount of carbon monoxide escapes, posing great danger. Tying a wet towel around the mouth and nose is the simplest way to prevent inhaling carbon monoxide. Any water can be used to wet the towel; it doesn't need to be offered to the gods.)

The axe used by Uncle Four to open the kiln had been passed down through generations in the charcoal gang. With a swift swing, the sealed kiln mouth was split open. Four teams, ready and waiting, quickly passed buckets of water to pour into the kiln at a very fast speed.

This was the most thrilling moment. Poisonous gas soared into the sky, and the sound of water pouring into the kiln was deafening. The participants moved swiftly and shouted continuously. The success of a kiln of charcoal depended on the coordination at this moment.

When the water was poured into the kiln and no more white gas emerged, the charcoal burning process was complete, and tens of thousands of pounds of fine charcoal could be removed from the kiln.

Through Fernsby's narration, I began to understand why the leader of the charcoal gang was called "Uncle Four." In the entire charcoal burning process, the number "four" was significant. Each piece of wood was four feet long. The charcoal kiln had four fire mouths. The wood was stacked into four layers in the kiln. It took four days and four nights to burn charcoal. Almost every step was associated with the number four. The respectful title of "Uncle Four" likely originated from this.

Fernsby's storytelling was a labyrinthine journey, filled with sprawling digressions that occasionally ventured into the realm of the divine—such as the time he spent nearly half an hour recounting his ritualistic reverence for deities, a detail that, while colorful, did little to illuminate the core narrative. Yet, in the tangle of his words, the essential knowledge of charcoal burning emerged, stark and utilitarian, stripped of the extraneous.

When Fernsby concluded his tale, the fundamentals of charcoal production were mine, as was the enigmatic origin of the moniker "Uncle Four." However, the most vital query remained shrouded in mystery—an omission so deliberate it seemed to hum with its own presence. What, indeed, was the peculiar significance of that particular piece of charcoal?

I sensed the imperative to probe further, yet intuition warned me against direct confrontation. Fernsby Three and Bian Five's reticence was palpable; they danced around the heart of the matter, dropping only vague hints of an occurrence—a ghost of an event that lingered unspoken. With careful thought, I devised a question designed to pierce the veil of their silence without appearing to do so overtly. "Was this piece of charcoal also produced under the circumstances you just described?" I asked.

The beauty of this question lay in its simplicity. Should the charcoal be ordinary, Fernsby need only affirm. Yet, should it conceal deeper secrets, he would be ensnared by the complexity of his own narrative, revealing through hesitation what his words sought to obscure. Thus, the stage was set for the unraveling of truth, hidden within the shadows of ambiguity.

As expected, the moment my question hung in the air, both Fernsby and Bian seemed momentarily paralyzed, as if caught in a temporal rift, their expressions oscillating between bewilderment and hesitation. Fernsby stammered, repeating, "This piece of charcoal—this piece of charcoal—this piece of charcoal—" as if the words themselves had become an incantation, a spell he couldn't quite complete.

Silence stretched between them, thick and impenetrable. Bian's face was a mask, devoid of any readable emotion, a stoic canvas that betrayed nothing of his internal thoughts. Meanwhile, Fernsby appeared visibly discomfited, as if grappling with a secret too cumbersome to bear alone.

I pressed on, unwilling to let the moment dissipate, convinced that the charcoal harbored some clandestine truth. "Mr. Bian," I ventured, "is it because of an accident—and—"

Bian Five flinched as if struck, a jolt of surprise breaking his composure. "Yes, I—disfigured," he confessed, an admission laden with unspoken history.

"You's a man, not a woman. A little disfigurement is not a big deal!" I replied, my words crafted to resonate with Bian's unvoiced insecurities, and they seemed to strike a chord. He responded with an unexpected gratitude, "Thank—thank you!"

Undeterred, I continued, "The accident must have been very unusual? Was it related to this piece of charcoal?"

Yet again, my inquiry was met with silence, a charged pause that conveyed more than words could articulate. Fernsby and Bian exchanged glances, a silent dialogue that I could only observe. Fernsby sighed, a weary sound that carried years of untold stories. "Mr. Morris, Miss Sallow, originally, we should tell you, but—but I don't know if Aunt Four is willing!"

Flora, who had remained silent until now, spoke with an authority that belied her previous quietude. Her words cut through the tension like a scalpel: "Of course Aunt Four agreed, otherwise, why would she let you two talk to us for so long?"

Their startled exclamations of "Ah" confirmed her insight had hit its mark. Fernsby, perhaps relieved, turned to Bian Five. "Bian, do you want me to say it, or would you prefer to tell it yourself?"?"

"You say it," Bian Five replied, conceding his role in this unfolding drama. "I don't speak very fluently, anyway. You were there when that person came!"

Fernsby nodded eagerly, as if the act of speaking might exorcise the shadows of the past. "Yes! Yes!"

My anticipation soared, acutely aware that I stood on the precipice of revelation. From Bian's words, it was already apparent that the matter involved a singular individual—someone whose presence was so potent that even now, the memory of it seemed to tremble within them. Fernsby's silence, filled with an unspoken terror, only deepened the mystery. I waited, giving him space to marshal his thoughts.

Finally, Fernsby began, his voice carrying the weight of years past. "That was many years ago."

Bian interjected, grounding the narrative in time. "It was the second year after Uncle Four took over."

"Yes, the second year," Fernsby echoed, allowing himself a moment's pause. "I still remember that day, Uncle Four opened seven kilns in one day. By the time the sun set, he was extremely tired. The hard work and tension of opening a kiln was really unbearable, even for a strong iron man!"

Bian again interjected, recalling the vivid hues of the past. "That day, when we accompanied Uncle Four back, the sun had just set, and the sky was red with clouds. I said to Uncle Four, 'Look at the sky. It might rain heavily tomorrow. We should seal the kilns as soon as possible!' I still remember that, as soon as I said that, Uncle Four immediately ordered several people to get it done!

Fernsby confirmed, "Yes, it was very hot and humid. We went to Uncle Four's house together—Mr. Morris, Miss Sallow, I tell you, Uncle Four's house in his hometown is exactly the same as this one!"

Flora and I nodded, acknowledging the detail, though the precision of their recollections bordered on excessive. Yet, in their meticulousness, the past unfurled with startling clarity.

Fernsby continued, painting the scene with his words. "We entered the door, and the brothers saluted us as usual. Suddenly, Lil Seven came over—"

I interjected, seeking clarity. "Who is Lil Seven?"

Bian provided context, "There are eight people in our gang who act as leaders, managing the affairs of each hall."

I nodded, signaling my understanding.

Bian elaborated, "I'm afraid you don't understand. The leader of the gang is Uncle Four. Fernsby Three can be ranked third because he has been in the gang for a long time and has made great contributions. There are no first or second rankings in the gang!"

As Bian delineated the hierarchy, Fernsby puffed up with pride, basking in the recognition of his station. I refrained from inquiring further into his "great contributions," suspecting that such tales would be lengthy and tinged with violence—a history I had no desire to explore.

Fernsby resumed, "Lil Seven came over and saluted Uncle Four. He looked unhappy: 'Uncle Four, there is a person who came this afternoon and has been waiting for you!' There are many people who often come from all over to see Uncle Four. Uncle also likes to make friends. When friends come, he never disappoints them. But that day, he was too tired. He hesitated for a moment and said to me: 'Fernsby, go and see him on my behalf. I want to rest!' Of course, I agreed. Lil Seven said again: 'That person is in the small living room!' The small living room is the one we are in now."

Flora and I shared a glance, the familiarity of the setting lending an eerie immediacy to their tale.

Fernsby pressed on, "After Uncle Four gave the order and entered the living room, he went upstairs directly. I, Bian Five, and Lil Seven. Bian, you found that Lil Seven's expression was a little bit off, right?"

Bian nodded, confirming the anomaly. "Yes, Lil Seven's expression was very off. Miss Sallow, you haven't seen Lil Seven? He is the most ruthless person in the gang. No matter how dangerous the matter is, he never frowns. He has been injured countless times and his body is full of scars! His nickname is Omega Supreme ."

I listened, a mix of amusement and disbelief at the mythic qualities attributed to "Lil Seven," a character seemingly plucked from the pages of a legend. Yet here he was, a living enigma.

Bian continued, "I saw Lil Seven, looking at the back of Uncle Four going up the stairs, he hesitated to speak, and seemed to be in a dilemma, so I asked: 'Lil Seven, what's the matter?' Lil Seven didn't answer me immediately, but pointed to the door of the small living room. I hurriedly said:

'Is the person who came here to cause trouble?' Mr. Morris, the power of the Charcoal Gang is great. It is natural that people will come to cause trouble from time to time. You know, it was the underworld!"

I nodded, acknowledging the truth of their world. "I understand that in those days, whoever had the strongest fist was the most ruthless!"

My words carried a hint of irony, but neither Fernsby nor Bian seemed to perceive it, their focus entirely on the narrative they were unraveling, a story that promised to reveal the hidden significance of the charcoal and the stranger in the small living room.

Bian continued, recalling the incident with a gravity that seemed to pull the room's attention into a singular focus. "Lil Seven remarked at the time, 'He doesn't seem like he's here to cause trouble, but there's definitely something odd about him.' Brother Three laughed and said, 'We'll know what kind of person he is when we see him.' I nodded, and the three of us stepped into the small living room."

As he spoke, Bian cast a sidelong glance at Fernsby. It was a true "A glance," for beneath his unique mask, only one of his eyes was visible—a lone window into his thoughts. That eye, filled with a perplexed and enigmatic expression, hinted at the enduring mystery of the man they encountered that day, a puzzle that had never quite resolved.

Fernsby picked up the thread of the narrative, his voice steady yet tinged with a hint of the past's shadow. "We all entered the small living room together, and immediately, we saw a man standing there, his back to the door, engrossed in examining a small incense burner on the corner table." He gestured towards a corner in the room, prompting me to look. Indeed, a table stood there, its placement identical to the one he described, as if frozen in time.

"As soon as we entered, Bian Five called out, 'Friend, are you from the crooked line or the straight line?'" Fernsby recounted.

Flora and I exchanged amused glances, recognizing the archaic "incision," a linguistic relic from the gangs of the River Forth Basin. This coded language, crafted to veil intentions and affiliations, was a tapestry of dialects rich enough to merit academic study. Bian's question was a subtle probe into the man's intentions—whether he came as a friend or foe.

Fernsby continued, "When Bian Five posed the question, the man turned around. His appearance took us all by surprise. He had a gentle demeanor, clad in a black decent suit, a copper basin hat resting on the table—clearly his own. He wore black leather shoes, though the country roads had stained them a muddy yellow. From his appearance, it was obvious he wasn't one of us."

I couldn't help but interject, "So he didn't understand Mr. Bian's words?"

Bian nodded, confirming, "Exactly, he was bewildered. He turned around, confusion etched on his face, and simply asked, 'What?' I laughed then and told the brother Three and brother Seven, 'He's a Empty One!'—a term for someone unaffiliated with any gang. The man then asked, 'Who is the uncle four of the Charcoal Gang?' His hands rubbed together in an anxious rhythm."

Fernsby continued, his tone still carrying the pride of past renown. "I told him, 'Uncle Four is exhausted today and doesn't wish to see anyone. If you have something to say, tell me. I'm Fernsby Three.' Mr. Morris, Miss Sallow, I told you, my name carries weight from north to south of Yorkshire. Yet, the man seemed impervious to my reputation. He merely muttered 'oh oh' and insisted, 'I need to see Uncle Four. He must decide, or else it may be too late! I fear it's already too late!' His urgency was infuriating, so I snapped, 'Speak your mind. I can make decisions here!'"

Bian picked up the narrative, his voice tinged with a lingering sense of awe. "Brother Three has the authority to make decisions on gang matters. But when the man heard this, he stepped forward and said, 'Mr. Fernsby, then please, the Autumn kiln hasn't been lit yet, can you open it?'"

The memory seemed to grip Bian, his hand clenching into a fist, his knuckles cracking in audible protest. Even after all these years, the stranger's request still resonated with a strange intensity.

Fernsby's expression mirrored Bian's tension, and I found myself intrigued by the gravity of such a seemingly innocuous request. "Mr. Morris, you might not grasp the significance," Fernsby explained, "On that day, Uncle Four had opened seven kilns, and I wasn't idle either. I handled the stacking for four kilns—Autumn, Harvest, Winter, and Storage. Our kilns are numbered according to the Thousand Character Classic."

The detail was unexpected, a curious intersection of tradition and superstition. Perhaps the Thousand Character Classic's structure, with its four-character phrases, appealed to "Uncle Four's" sensibilities.

I nodded thoughtfully, "The request does seem unusual, but—"

Before I could finish, Fernsby interrupted, his voice rising with fervor. "Once the wood is stacked and the kiln sealed, we wait for the auspicious time to ignite it. That day, the auspicious hour had been set for six o'clock in the morning. Once sealed, the kiln cannot be opened!"

Flora and I spoke in unison, "Why not?"

Fernsby's answer was emphatic. "It's the rule!" His face flushed with the weight of tradition. "Once a kiln is sealed, it stays sealed until the charcoal is ready. That's the rule!"

I inhaled deeply, trying to understand. "What happens if you reopen a sealed kiln before lighting it?"

At my question, Bian's single eye widened in surprise, while Fernsby waved his hand as if brushing away an unpleasant thought. "You simply don't do it, and—no one ever has!"

Flora nudged me gently, signaling to let the matter rest. I obliged, recognizing the futility of seeking logic in the realm of "rules." The stranger's request, the insistence on breaking a deeply ingrained tradition, hinted at layers of meaning and consequence we had yet to uncover. As I pondered this, the story of the mysterious visitor and the unopened kiln loomed larger, casting shadows across the simple act of burning charcoal.

Chapter 5

Stranger's Strange
Demands and Actions

In the charged silence that followed, I watched Bian and Fernsby as the excitement from their retelling gradually subsided. Eventually, Fernsby picked up the thread, recounting with a mix of disbelief and lingering frustration. "The man's request left us all stunned. Within the Charcoal Gang, such a demand was unthinkable, almost heretical. It felt as though he was deliberately stirring trouble. Brother Seven, being young and hot-headed, reacted instantly. He seized the man's arm, challenging him, 'You come to make trouble, show your skills!' Brother Seven was a master of grappling, and he moved with the confidence of someone expecting resistance. With a twist, his grip was meant to incapacitate."

At this point, I interjected, "I suppose the stranger's arm was dislocated, then?"

Both Fernsby and Bian stared at me, startled. "Mr. Morris, do you know this person?" they asked.

I shook my head, "No, I don't. But from how you've described him, it's clear this man was no martial artist. Without martial training, Lil Seven's Tiger Claw technique would be devastating. The man was bound to get hurt."

Bian Five sighed, the memory still vivid. "Exactly. The man knew nothing of martial arts. There was a snap, and the stranger's arm was out of joint. Even Brother Seven seemed taken aback. The man's face went pale with pain. Brother Three intervened quickly, chiding, 'Brother Seven, fix his arm. A guest is still a guest, we can't be so reckless!' It was an attempt to smooth over the incident. Brother Seven, regaining his composure, reset the man's arm, though the stranger was left speechless from the pain. Brother Three, ever cautious, reassured him, 'Friend, forget what you said. It's a gang taboo. Although you're an Empty One, if the other gang brothers hear, we can't promise your safety.' The man, in tears, remained silent for a long while."

Fernsby continued, recounting their initial assumptions about the stranger. "We thought he'd drop the matter. I suspected he was sent by someone to cause trouble, and I hoped to coax out who had sent him. But once he regained his composure, he repeated his plea, 'Please, open the Autumn kiln. It's crucial!'"

Fernsby paused, then continued, " At that moment, Brother Five, unable to contain himself, had responded harshly, 'Shut your mouth, or I'll take your head off!' Despite his frailty, the man remained resolute, 'Even if you do, please honor my request.'"

The stranger's unwavering determination piqued my curiosity. "What did he hope to achieve by opening the kiln?"

"Good question," Fernsby replied. "His resolve suggested something significant was at stake, even if it meant risking his life."

Flora added, "Perhaps he thought you were bluffing."

Fernsby glanced at Bian, who silently picked up a tin can from the table and crushed it effortlessly, the metal yielding like paper. The gesture conveyed a silent threat. Back then, with both hands, Bian must have demonstrated his formidable strength, making it clear he could carry out his threat with ease. Yet, the stranger's lack of fear only deepened their intrigue.

Fernsby continued, "I asked him directly, 'What do you need from the kiln?' He replied that he needed to retrieve something important—a mere piece of wood. Brother Seven scoffed, 'Nothing important is in the kiln, just wood!' The stranger insisted, 'It's a specific piece of wood.'"

At this, Fernsby sighed deeply, and Flora and I exchanged puzzled glances. The stranger's insistence on retrieving a commonplace item—a piece of wood no less—seemed absurd, especially given the lengths he was willing to go.

Bian Five picked up where Fernsby left off, "Our shouting must have reached Uncle Four. He entered the room, assessing the situation with a frown. 'What's all this commotion? Who is he?' Brother Seven explained the stranger's request, and Uncle Four's displeasure was immediate. He addressed the man sternly, 'What's wrong with you?' The man responded, 'Please, I just need to take back a piece of wood.' Uncle Four demanded, 'What wood? Be specific!'"

Fernsby nodded, his eyes distant, as if replaying the scene in his mind. "The image is still vivid," he mused, tracing the air with his finger as if the table were before him. "When Uncle Four questioned him, the man approached a table where a small black suitcase lay. Our tension was palpable, fearing he might produce something alarming. Yet, all he retrieved was a paper bag, from which he extracted a bundle of folded papers."

Bian chimed in, echoing the strangeness of the moment. "Indeed, it was peculiar. We were clueless about his intentions. He unfolded the papers and spread them out, inviting us, 'Please look here.' We stepped closer, drawn to the circles and writing covering the sheet. It resembled a map."

Fernsby affirmed, "It was a map. The man spoke with an uncanny familiarity about Yorkshire's terrain, more so than I possessed. Pointing to a circle, he identified it as 'Ashfield.' I was taken aback—Ashfield is a remote valley, known only to locals. Yet, this stranger named it without hesitation. He continued, 'The forest north of here has been cleared.' Brother Seven, ever the skeptic, confirmed, 'Yes, that was last month.'"

Sighing deeply, Fernsby recounted the man's lament, "He sighed heavily, 'If I had arrived a month or even a day earlier, this might have been avoided!' Uncle Four, losing patience, demanded clarity, 'What do you want?' The man explained, 'A specific tree in that forest was felled. I tracked it to the east field, where it was stored. This morning, it was loaded into the Autumn kiln.' Uncle Four turned to me for confirmation. I shrugged, 'Wood is wood. How can you be sure your tree is in the Autumn kiln?" The man's response was cryptic."

Bian recalled, "He insisted, 'I know, I know it's in the Autumn kiln. Please, just let me retrieve it, and I'll go.' Miss Sallow, you can imagine our dilemma—what were we to do with such insistence?"

Flora offered a practical solution, "Naturally, you should ask him what made that wood or tree so special."

Fernsby nodded, "Uncle Four did inquire, but the man remained evasive, his demeanor increasingly odd. Frustrated, Uncle Four ordered, 'Brother Seven, this man is unhinged, remove him!' Brother Seven had been anticipating this directive. He grabbed the man's wrist, then his collar, and unceremoniously escorted him out. In the commotion, the man left his suitcase behind, an oversight we assumed he'd rectify by returning for it."

Fernsby and Bian's detailed account left me intrigued but no closer to understanding the deeper narrative. The stranger's peculiar behavior and unyielding focus on a single piece of wood painted an enigmatic picture. I asked, "Did the stranger ever return?"

The room was heavy with silence as Fernsby and Bian Five grappled with the memories of that fateful day. Fernsby's voice wavered, the tension of the past creeping into the present. "We were busy with our gang duties and didn't dwell on the stranger. After dinner, Brother Five, Uncle Four, and I inspected the kilns. Fourteen kilns stood ready, their firewood stacked meticulously. The auspicious hour in the morning approached, heightening our nerves. Every detail had to be perfect."

He hesitated, his voice catching as he continued, "Then, suddenly—" He faltered, turning to Bian Five for support.

Bian Five picked up the story, his words taut with urgency. "Someone shouted near the Autumn Kiln. We rushed over to find that madman scaling the kiln, his determination palpable. He had an axe strapped to his back, clearly intending to breach the kiln's seal. Such an act was unheard of in the Charcoal Gang. We yelled for him to come down, but he ignored us, continuing his climb."

Fernsby interjected, his breath steadying as he spoke. "Uncle Four, anxious, ordered Brother Five to stop him. Brother Five quickly ascended, but the man had already reached the top. There was a hole there, and he plunged through it just as the gong struck. The auspicious time had arrived!"

I interrupted, needing clarification, "Wait, what does the auspicious time mean?"

Flora's voice was a whisper, "It's the precise moment when the fire must be lit."

Fernsby nodded, "Yes, the pyrotechnicians stood ready with torches, awaiting the signal."

A chill ran through me. "But someone had just jumped into the kiln!"

Fernsby swallowed hard, "Yes, and the pyrotechnician hesitated, looking to Uncle Four for direction. The gong continued its toll—once, twice, thrice. With only four strikes, time was slipping away. Uncle Four decided, 'Throw the fire!'"

I rose to my feet, shocked and angry. "You—you intended to burn a man alive?"

Fernsby met my gaze, unflinching. "Uncle Four saw Lil Five climbing and knew he could rescue the man without missing the time."

Flora squeezed my hand, sharing my disbelief.

Fernsby continued, "Lil Five's skills were unmatched. He could save the man and not disrupt the auspicious hour."

Suppressing my frustration, I listened as Fernsby described the scene. "The torch was cast into the kiln's heart, and Brother Five followed through the top. Silence fell over us. Brother Five, do you remember how long you were inside?"

The room was thick with the weight of the past, each word from Bian and Fernsby adding layers to the haunting tableau they painted. Bian's recounting of the harrowing moment was still, remarkably, steady. "I don't know how long I was inside. The fire surrounded me instantly, the kiln's four fire ports ensuring no escape. Smoke and flames blinded me. I climbed out without understanding how."

Fernsby, however, was gripped by a visceral emotion that seemed to transport him back to that perilous moment. His voice was charged with a mix of fear and disbelief as he described the aftermath of Bian's leap into the inferno. "When Brother Five jumped in, we rushed to aid him. Reaching the top, I saw a hand emerge from the kiln's opening. I grabbed it, desperate to pull him out."

His expression twisted with terror, Fernsby's gaze fell to the floor as he moved to a corner, his back to us. His shoulders quaked, a sob escaping—a sound that spoke of a trauma too deep to be silenced by time.

The shock of Fernsby's reaction was palpable. Bian Five, though pale, retained a calm demeanor, offering quiet reassurance, "Brother Three, it's in the past. Don't dwell on it."

Fernsby drew a shaky breath, turning to face us, his hand gesturing to Bian's empty sleeve. His voice quivered, "I reached out and grasped that hand, intending to pull him out. But then—" His voice cracked, "I pulled with all my strength, and I lost my balance. I tumbled backward down the kiln."

The story seemed to demand every ounce of Fernsby's courage to continue. His breaths came in shallow gasps as he relived the horror. "I thought I had Brother Five. But when I looked, I was holding only his arm. The force of my pull—I'd torn his arm off. I screamed—"

The scream Fernsby let out now was a mere echo of the one he described—a sound that must have been filled with unimaginable horror and disbelief.

Covering his face, Fernsby's body shuddered violently, lost in the memory of a night where the boundaries between life and death blurred in the glow of kiln fires. The room sat in stunned silence, the gravity of the tale hanging in the air like smoke from a long-extinguished fire, a testament to the enduring scars left by that night and the mysterious stranger who had ignited such chaos.

The room was enveloped in an uneasy silence, each of us processing the gravity of the story. Even though I hadn't been there, Fernsby's account painted a vivid picture of chaos and desperation near the Autumn charcoal kiln. The scene must have been harrowing, with emotions running high as survival instincts clashed with the unthinkable.

Flora, ever the voice of reason and empathy, quickly reassured Fernsby, "Uncle Three, Uncle Five must have been injured before you pulled. There's no way you could have torn his arm off without it already being compromised."

Bian Five nodded, his demeanor remarkably composed despite the grim topic. "That's right. I've always assured him that the injury occurred in the kiln. The flames were intense; I believe my arm was severely burned. In my rush to escape, I felt no pain. Brother Three's pull merely detached what was already damaged."

His calmness in recounting such a traumatic event was admirable. There was a resilience about him, a stoic acceptance of what had happened, as if he had long come to terms with the past and its irreversible consequences.

Fernsby lowered his hands, his face etched with regret and sorrow. "Brother Five, I hurt you," he said, his voice laden with remorse.

Bian Five's recounting was both haunting and heroic. "You saved me, Brother Three. Though I lost my arm when you pulled me, that action also lifted me upward. Brother Seven grabbed my hair to stop me from falling, and then Uncle Four managed to drag me out by the shoulder."

Fernsby swallowed, his voice thick with emotion. "When I realized I was holding only your arm, I looked up and saw Brother Seven and Uncle Four pulling you out. I even heard you scream."

Bian Five nodded, his calm acceptance of the past starkly evident. "Yes, I was conscious when I emerged from the kiln, and when the outside air hit me, the pain was overwhelming. I screamed, then blacked out."

Fernsby continued, his tone steadying. "I jumped up to help. By then, Uncle Four and others had brought you down. Your shoulder was burned, exposing the bone. There was no blood, just charred flesh."

The description painted a vivid picture of the horror Bian Five had endured. Despite the brevity of his exposure to the flames, the injuries were catastrophic. The fact that he survived at all seemed miraculous.

Bian Five spoke with a certain grim humor, "According to Uncle Four, I was unconscious for half a month before waking. Surviving was sheer luck, really."

His words carried the weight of someone who had faced death and lived to tell the tale. We all sat in reflective silence, the severity of his injuries serving as a sobering reminder of the kiln's danger.

I remarked, "It's fortunate only one side was burned."

Bian Five explained, "The Charcoal Gang has extensive experience with treating burns. We have unique remedies. As long as the burns aren't too severe, healing is possible."

I nodded, aware of the gang's close ties with fire and the inevitable risks involved. Over time, they would have developed effective treatments for burns.

As Fernsby calmed, the silence that followed was heavy with unspoken thoughts. I, too, found myself lost in the imagined chaos of that day. Then, a question struck me. "The stranger—Mr. Bian went in after him, but what happened to him?"

The answer was already clear in my mind. Given the stranger's lack of skills and the perilous nature of the kiln, his fate seemed inevitable. Fernsby and Bian Five's prolonged silence confirmed my suspicion.

Finally, Fernsby spoke, his voice steady but somber. "The stranger perished in the kiln."

Though expected, the confirmation was still unsettling. I wanted to voice my frustration, perhaps blame them for the stranger's death, but the sight of Bian Five, who had paid dearly for his bravery, tempered my judgment. The tragedy seemed rooted not in malice but in the weight of tradition and superstition that had enveloped the Charcoal Gang for generations.

I sighed, the complexity of the situation pressing heavily on me. "What happened next? Were there any new developments?"

The story hung in the air, incomplete yet rich with lessons about the perils of tradition, the unpredictability of fate, and the enduring strength of those who face such trials.

Fernsby's recounting of the aftermath was intense, his voice tinged with a mixture of regret and frustration. "I jumped up to help, but by then, they had already taken Brother Five down. In my panic, I tried to reattach his severed arm as if sheer will could make it whole again. It took several brothers to pull me away, and they hurried Brother

Five off for treatment. Amid this chaos, someone shouted about the kiln roof, and I looked up to see a pillar of fire shooting skyward through the opening."

Bian Five elaborated, describing the desperate strength of the stranger. "On top of the kiln, after it was sealed, there was only a small opening. But somehow, the man had managed to break through the thick sealing with his feet, creating a larger hole. He jumped through it, and so did I."

Fernsby continued, "Because of the larger hole, the fire found a path and roared out like a dragon. Someone scrambled up to seal it with wet mud, reducing it back to a small opening."

I leaned forward, about to question their lack of effort to save the stranger, but Flora, perceptive as ever, voiced what was on my mind. "Even if you had the best fireproof gear and were there, what could you have done?"

Her question silenced my criticism. The reality was stark: under those conditions, even if I had been equipped to withstand the flames, the stranger would have already been beyond help. Entering the kiln would have been futile.

I swallowed my words, acknowledging the futility with a silent nod. Fernsby, sensing my internal struggle, resumed his account. "While Uncle Four was focused on treating

Brother Five, who was still unconscious, I went back with him to his quarters. It was nearly dawn by then. We gathered in the small living room, where Aunt Four joined us briefly, understanding something grave had happened, though she wasn't involved in kiln matters. Her presence was comforting, but she soon left. Uncle Four sat in silence, and a heavy gloom settled over us."

Fernsby paused, reflecting on the tension in the room before continuing. "After a while, Brother Seven, ever blunt, cursed the situation. 'Where did that madman come from? Was he really after a piece of wood? How could someone die for wood?' His question hung unanswered. Then I noticed the stranger's small suitcase. It was our only lead to understanding the enigma he'd left behind. I suggested to Uncle Four that we open it, hoping for clues. Uncle Four, weary and frustrated, nodded his consent."

With a heavy sigh, Fernsby recounted, "I unlocked the suitcase. Inside, there were only a few old clothes. I searched further and found some items in the lid's pocket: tickets, some money, and a piece of paper with writing on it."

The room was silent, each of us waiting for him to reveal what was written, sensing that whatever was on that paper might hold answers to the stranger's desperate actions and perhaps, the wood he sought so fervently.

Fernsby's revelation was startling. "It seemed as if he anticipated something might go wrong. On that paper, he had written his full name, his origin, and his profession."

Bian Five murmured, "We initially assumed he was there to cause trouble, but it turns out that wasn't the case at all."

Curiosity piqued, I asked, "Who was this man?"

Fernsby explained, "His name was Dingle Asim, hailing from Whitby. He was the principal of a primary school there."

The information left me bewildered. The notion of a primary school principal from a small city making his way to charcoal gang for a piece of wood seemed bizarre beyond belief.

Fernsby's expression mirrored my incredulity. "We were all taken aback, unsure if the paper's contents were genuine. Uncle Four was silent for a moment, then carefully folded the paper and decided, 'Once this batch of kilns is opened, I'll head to Whitby. Brother Three, you'll manage the gang affairs in my absence.' I reassured him, 'Fourth Uncle, don't worry about these matters.' But Uncle Four insisted, 'Fernsby, this is too peculiar, and it involves a human life. Dingle Asim must have family. I need to inform them personally.' Brother Seven suggested, 'Just send someone,' but Uncle Four was adamant about going himself."

Listening to this, I sighed, "Mr. Fernsby, do you understand Uncle Four's intentions?"

Fernsby's recollection of the days following the incident was heavy with unease. "Uncle Four was deeply saddened because he had given the order to light the fire after the man had jumped in. But at that moment, it seemed unavoidable. I think he carried that weight with him."

The Charcoal Gang felt the impact profoundly. Fernsby described a pervasive silence among the members, an unspoken agreement to avoid discussing the incident. Conversations were sparse, often drowned out by alcohol-induced stupors that led to frequent altercations. It was a community trying to cope with an unsettling event that few could understand or articulate.

As the fourth day approached, it was time to open the kilns. The usual anticipation was tinged with dread, particularly regarding the Autumn kiln, which everyone agreed should be addressed last. Fernsby's demeanor turned tense as he recounted climbing to the top of the Autumn kiln with Uncle Four, both of them taking precautions by covering their faces with wet towels. Uncle Four, with a somber resolve, muttered a quiet invocation before striking the kiln's seal with his axe.

The sudden "boom" that erupted from the kiln as the seal was broken was unexpected and alarming. Instead of the anticipated gases, a plume of snow-white ash shot upwards—a sign of a kiln explosion, the worst kind of disaster. The realization struck Fernsby and the others with a chilling finality.

Bian Five explained the gravity of the situation. "A kiln explosion means the wood inside has been completely reduced to ash, and it's considered extremely unlucky. The kiln becomes unusable after such an event. It's been decades since anything like this has happened."

As the ash settled, Fernsby described how they were covered in it, though thankfully unharmed due to the cooling effect of the wind. The Water Dragon Team took action, pouring water into the kiln to quell the eruption of ash, signaling the end of the Autumn kiln's utility.

I pressed for more details, especially about Dingle Asim, the stranger whose actions precipitated the calamity. Fernsby, however, spoke instead about Uncle Four's departure the following day. "Uncle Four left alone to Whitby. He felt it was his responsibility to face Dingle Asim's family. In his absence, I managed the gang, ensuring no one approached the Autumn kiln. Despite my concerns, things remained calm. We had several successful kiln openings, and Brother Five, although severely injured, eventually regained consciousness."

The story left me with a sense of unresolved mystery. Dingle's motivations remained elusive, shrouded in the ashes of the Autumn kiln and the silence of those who witnessed the inexplicable events. The Charcoal Gang continued, but the shadow of those days lingered, a reminder of the strange and tragic intersection of lives and the unknown forces that sometimes shape them.

I listened intently, anticipation building as I waited for Fernsby to reveal the outcome of Uncle Four's mysterious journey. Fernsby continued, his voice carrying the weight of untold stories: "Uncle Four was gone for nearly a month. Upon his return, he took one look at Brother Five's injuries and pulled me into this room. His expression was grave. 'Brother Three,' he said, 'I need your help with something.' In the gang, our loyalty was bound by an oath—an unbreakable promise to follow Uncle Four through fire and water. He could have ordered me to do things, but he consulted me, so it had to be something truly extraordinary."

I couldn't hold back any longer. "Wait, Mr. Fernsby," I interrupted, urgency in my voice. "Did Uncle Four say if he met Dingle Asim's family in Whitby? Why was he gone for an entire month?"

Fernsby took a deep breath, hesitating for a moment. "No, he didn't mention it. He seemed troubled, so I didn't press him for details."

He paused, noting my curiosity, and gestured to silence my questions. "Whatever Uncle Four did during that month, he never spoke of it. I never discovered what it was."

The mystery hung in the air, thick and impenetrable. My mind raced with possibilities. What had Uncle Four encountered that compelled him to silence? What secrets did that month hold?

The enigma only deepened, leaving me with more questions than answers. What could have happened in Whitby that Uncle Four couldn't—or wouldn't—share with us? The silence was a puzzle in itself, a tantalizing riddle waiting to be solved.

"This doesn't seem right," I remarked, my curiosity piqued. "Why didn't Uncle Four mention anything about his trip?"

Fernsby shook his head, a shadow of uncertainty crossing his face. "I don't know either. It wasn't until Brother Five was mostly healed and could move around that he brought it up with Uncle Four."

Fernsby exchanged a glance with Bian, who nodded in confirmation. "Yes, I assumed Uncle Four had handled something important in Whitby and had shared it with the others while I was incapacitated. One night, as six or seven of us were gathered, I asked offhandedly, 'Uncle Four, did you meet the Dingle family? What exactly is Mr. Dingle involved in?' The question hung in the air, and Uncle Four's reaction was immediate clouded."

Fernsby picked up the thread of the story, his voice lowering as if the memory itself demanded reverence. "Uncle Four's face darkened instantly, an expression none of us had ever seen before. We all wanted to probe further, but fear held us back. When Brother Five asked, it was as if the room collectively held its breath, waiting for Uncle Four's response. Seeing his expression, we knew Brother Five had inadvertently touched a nerve."

Bian Five added, "Realizing my mistake, I was at a loss. After a long pause, Uncle Four finally admitted, 'Azim Dingle had a young son, unaware of his father's fate. I left him enough money to live comfortably.' That spoke volumes about Uncle Four's generosity. He then instructed us never to mention the matter again, and we respected his wishes."

The revelation that Mr. Dingle's son was taken care of financially hinted at Uncle Four's sense of responsibility and compassion. Yet, it left many questions unanswered. What exactly had Uncle Four discovered or done during his month away? What was the true story behind Dingle Asim's actions?

I pondered these questions, wondering about the untold story. Then, I asked Fernsby about the task Uncle Four had given him upon returning.

Fernsby explained, "I told Uncle Four I'd do whatever he needed. He looked at me and said, ' Fernsby, I want you to come with me to the Autumn charcoal kiln.' His request stunned me. What could he possibly be looking for in the kiln? Azim Dingle's remains would have been obliterated. The kiln was filled with ash after the explosion, blocking the entrance. Entering from the top would be perilous, as the ash could suffocate anyone who sank into it."

The risks were clear, yet Uncle Four's determination suggested there was something he believed needed to be confronted or discovered within the kiln. The nature of his quest remained a mystery, one that seemed entwined with the enigmatic circumstances surrounding Dingle's death and the events that followed.

CHAPTER 6

Stranger's Son
Interested in Charcoal

I nodded, sensing the gravity of the situation they had faced. The peril was tangible, almost as if I could feel the cold, oppressive air of the kiln myself.

Fernsby's breathing quickened as he recounted the story. "At that moment, I couldn't help but ask, 'Uncle Four, why?' His response was grave: 'Fernsby, don't question it. I need you to come with me. Alone, I might not make it out.' I protested, 'Brother Five has suffered enough because of Dingle's actions. We owe him nothing!'"

But Uncle Four was resolute. "'I must go,' he insisted, 'and only you can help me.' Reluctantly, I agreed. 'Alright, let's do this,' I said. Uncle Four nodded affirmatively, and I prepared, gathering a sturdy length of rope."

Fernsby's expression turned peculiar as he continued. "Together, we approached the Autumn Kiln. After the kiln explosion, the area was deserted, eerily silent. We climbed to the kiln's summit. I lit a pair of torches, tied the rope around Fourth Uncle and myself, and secured it to the kiln's roof. I went in first, with Uncle Four right behind. We descended into the kiln through the opening at the top."

As Fernsby spoke, his expression grew stranger, and he paused frequently. "Descending into the kiln, the torchlight revealed a smooth blanket of ash below, like untouched snow. I had calculated the rope's length, but misjudged by two feet, causing us to sink into the ash. The torchlight revealed something that made us both scream—a sound that echoed ominously in the kiln, stirring a swirling cloud of gray. But what truly caught our eyes was a solitary piece of charcoal sitting atop the ash, half-buried, half-exposed."

I was taken aback. "Is it the same piece?" I asked, almost involuntarily.

Fernsby confirmed, "Yes, it's this piece."

As I processed Fernsby's narrative, it was clear to me that the story was not a fabrication. The vivid details, the tension, the strangeness of it all—it was too real to be concocted. This piece of charcoal was undeniably special.

For one, it was linked to a mysterious and extraordinary event. While I knew of the external circumstances, the internal causes remained elusive. After the kiln explosion, logic dictated that all wood inside should have turned to ash; no charcoal should have survived.

I glanced at Fernsby, seeking more from his expression. He continued, "I was bewildered—how could a piece of charcoal remain in the ash? But Uncle Four, upon seeing it, seemed unfazed, almost as if he had expected it. He maneuvered toward the charcoal with great effort, seized it, and declared, 'Brother, let's head back up!' I couldn't resist asking, 'Uncle, did you anticipate finding charcoal in this kiln?'"

Fernsby stopped, the tale hanging in the air, leaving me on the edge of my seat, eager to hear the answer that Uncle Four might have given—or perhaps chose not to give.

Flora and I leaned forward, anticipation hanging thick in the air. "What did Uncle Four say?" we pressed, eager to unravel the mystery.

Fernsby hesitated, his brow furrowed in contemplation. "I still don't quite grasp Uncle Four's words," he admitted. "Even after discussing it with the gang brothers, we couldn't decipher his meaning."

Impatience tingled in my veins. "What did he say?" I urged, sensing the weight of a revelation.

Fernsby recounted Uncle Four's cryptic message: " He said, 'no, I didn't know there would be a piece of charcoal, but I knew there must be something in the kiln, so I went in to retrieve it.'"

His eyes locked onto mine, silently asking if I could unravel the enigma behind those words. I shook my head, the puzzle eluding me still. I turned to Flora, seeking insight.

Flora pondered briefly, then ventured, "Perhaps when Uncle Four reached Whitby, he stumbled upon something that made him certain there was an object of significance in the kiln. That drove him to retrieve it upon his return."

I interjected, "But isn't it expected that charcoal would be in a charcoal kiln—"

Flora cut me off, urgency in her voice. "Don't forget, something happened in that kiln!"

Silence stretched between us, the implications heavy with unspoken possibilities.

Fernsby continued, "Uncle Four and I left the kiln together, and he cautioned me to keep this secret. So—"

His gaze shifted apologetically to Bian Five. "Brother Five only learned about this piece of charcoal a few years ago.

Initially, only Uncle Four, Aunt Four, and I were aware. Uncle Four crafted a meticulous box for it, and Aunt Four has safeguarded it ever since. I don't understand its significance, but it must be vital."

I pressed, "How can you be so sure?"

Fernsby replied, "When circumstances forced us from our homeland, Uncle Four stayed behind, asking only Brother Five and me to accompany Aunt Four. She carried many valuables, but as we parted, Uncle Four pulled me aside. He said, 'Fernsby, Aunt Four holds many treasures, but remember, if calamity strikes, you can afford to lose anything—except that piece of charcoal..'"

The clarity of Fernsby's words resonated deeply. Uncle Four's insistence highlighted the charcoal's extraordinary importance.

Fernsby added, "I'm uncertain about Uncle Four's assurance to Aunt Four that it could be traded for its volume in gold. He must have confided more in her."

I lifted the charcoal from its box, letting the light play across its surface, searching for answers hidden in its dark depths.

No matter how you turned it, examined it, or pondered over it, this piece of charcoal was just that—an ordinary, unremarkable piece. Yet, beneath its soot-streaked exterior lay a labyrinth of secrets waiting to be unraveled.

Flora, ever more meticulous than I, probed further. "Uncle Three," she began, her voice steady and probing, "you mentioned that within the Charcoal Gang, only three individuals were privy to this piece's existence. But outside of the gang, is there anyone else who might know of it?"

Fernsby's response was immediate, a certainty ringing through his words. "Of course, there are others who know!"

His confidence intrigued me, though its source was a mystery. Fernsby elaborated, "Upon our arrival here, Aunt Four erected this very house and secured the land it stands on. She brought with her a trove of treasures—items of considerable worth. Yet, as time wore on, her wealth dwindled, consumed by the needs of those who followed. Jewelry and antiques were sold, piece by piece, until nothing remained. It was then that Aunt Four approached me and Brother Five, clutching the charcoal as if it were a relic, repeating what Uncle Four had confided to her."

Bian Five interjected, "That was the first I heard of this mysterious charcoal. The notion that it could be traded for gold seemed absurd. But Brother Three shared its origins, and Aunt Four reiterated, 'Uncle Four instructed me that should we find ourselves desperate, this charcoal could be sold, but only for its volume in gold.' After much deliberation, Brother Three and I resolved to place an advertisement in the paper."

Bian Five recounted that initial foray into the public eye—a venture I had missed, likely due to my absence from town. They had cast their net wide, hoping for a bite. And bite it did, for soon after, whispers of negotiation began to surface.

I leaned in, curiosity piqued. "Who reached out after the announcement ran?"

Bian Five continued, "For three days, the ad sat idle, unanswered. Anxiety gnawed at us. I turned to Brother Three, voicing my doubts, 'Could Aunt Four have been mistaken? How could one equate the worth of charcoal to that of gold?' Brother Three, unwavering, replied, 'Aunt Four is meticulous, especially with matters of such gravity. She's managed countless intricate affairs for the gang. Patience, let us wait two more days.'"

Fernsby inhaled deeply, a pause laden with suspense. "Indeed, I advised Brother Five to exercise patience, though I harbored my own doubts. But then, on the second day, the call came. The voice on the line was—was—"

The story hung like a pendulum, its momentum building, poised on the brink of revelation.

Fernsby's eyes locked with Bian Five's, a silent understanding passing between them before Bian Five spoke up. "I answered the call," he recounted, "The voice on the other end, a man who claimed his surname was Dingle, expressed a keen interest in the charcoal advertisement. He insisted on meeting in person to discuss further. I remember telling him, 'Meeting won't suffice unless you agree to our terms.' His response was quick, 'I agree, but there are matters best discussed face-to-face.' As I spoke with him, Brother Three joined me, and I asked the man to hold while we conferred."

Fernsby took over, his voice steady, "Brother Five relayed the man's request, and I saw no issue. The man said he would come immediately."

He paused, drawing in a breath before continuing, "After we hung up, Brother Five and I informed Aunt Four. Her response was one of moving resignation. 'I've never understood the significance of this charcoal,' she confessed, 'but Uncle Four entrusted it to me with such gravity. There must be a reason.' Despite her sorrow, she conceded, 'Since someone desires it and we are in need, what choice do we have?" We were left reflecting on the past, a silence filled with shared memories and unspoken regrets."

Bian Five added, "Back then, circumstances hadn't yet grown as dire. We still had a few helpers around. So when our guest arrived, it wasn't Brother Three and I who ushered him in."

He spoke deliberately, ensuring we grasped the context of their encounter with the enigmatic Mr. Dingle. I nodded, acknowledging the gravity of the moment. Bian Five continued, "Brother Three and I were with Aunt Four, reminiscing, until someone called from downstairs announcing the arrival of our guest. We descended together, entering the small living room—right here, in fact. Upon entering, what we saw froze us in our tracks."

His face twitched with the memory, an expression of surprise and something verging on fear. Fernsby's expression mirrored his. They fell silent, as if reliving the moment. Fernsby finally spoke, pointing to a corner, "The man stood there, his back to the door, studying a painting on the wall. Back then, the walls were adorned with calligraphy and art. His attire was ordinary, but his back—it was unmistakable."

Confused, I asked, "What was so distinct about his back?"

Flora, with her sharp intuition, interjected, "Could it be that his back resembled Asim Dingle, the one who caused trouble for the Charcoal Gang years ago?"

Fernsby nodded fervently, "Exactly!"

Flora pressed further, "And this man's surname is also Dingle. Could there be a connection to Asim Dingle?"

Fernsby and Bian Five exchanged a look of admiration. Fernsby replied, "Miss Sallow, just listen."

Flora nodded, and we both lapsed into silence, letting Fernsby continue. "Brother Five and I were taken aback. The man turned, and as he faced us, the resemblance was uncanny. Before us stood Asim Dingle, unchanged by time, save for his clothes."

Fernsby's breath hitched, his gaze seeking Bian Five's confirmation. Bian Five nodded, "Indeed. I exclaimed, 'So you survived the charcoal kiln!' But his bewilderment was immediate, and I realized my error. Azim Dingle couldn't have remained so young. I quickly redirected, 'Are you interested in exchanging gold for our charcoal?' My question, though abrupt, served to mask my initial outburst."

Fernsby picked up the thread, "The man was forthright. 'My name is Isaam Dingle,' he said, 'I saw your advertisement and hurried back from Scotland, where I conduct business.

May I see the charcoal?' It was a reasonable request, one we couldn't deny. I signaled to Brother Five, who went to fetch the charcoal from Aunt Four. I stayed, engaging Mr. Dingle in conversation."

He paused, rubbing his face as if to steady himself. "As we talked, his resemblance to Azim Dingle grew more apparent. I couldn't help asking, 'Mr. Dingle, are you from — ?' Isaam Dingle interrupted, 'Whitby. A modest place,' he said. I was startled, 'There was once a Mr. Dingle there—' At this, Isaam Dingle stood abruptly, 'That was my father. Did you know him?'"

Fernsby glanced at Flora and me, a bitter smile playing on his lips. "Imagine my surprise when he asked that. How would you respond?"

I murmured, "That was a delicate situation. It seemed Isaam Dingle was unaware of how his father died."

Fernsby nodded, "Correct! Though we bear no responsibility for Azim Dingle's death, the topic remains sensitive. I mumbled, 'Yes, we met a few times.' Isaam Dingle sighed, 'I was very young when my father died, I have no memory of him.'"

Flora added, "Indeed, Uncle Four remarked upon Azim Dingle's young son and even provided them financial support."

Fernsby agreed, "Yes, though we never knew what Uncle Four did in Whitby."

I pondered aloud, "There must be a reason Isaam Dingle seeks to trade gold for this charcoal. It can't be mere coincidence."

Fernsby concurred, "Yes, that was my thought. I asked him, 'Mr. Dingle, forgive my curiosity, but why are you keen on this exchange?' Isaam Dingle appeared puzzled, 'I honestly don't know,' he replied."

I couldn't help but question, "Is that plausible? Surely he must have a reason!"

Fernsby looked perplexed as he recounted the moment. "He quickly explained, 'My mother sent me here!' That was all he said, and then Bother Five returned with the charcoal."

Bian Five picked up the narrative. "I entered with the wooden box containing the charcoal, only to find Brother Three looking quite troubled. Unaware of what had transpired, I placed the box on the table, opening it to reveal the charcoal. Isaam Dingle's eyes widened in surprise. 'It's so large!' he exclaimed, his face a picture of confusion. 'I didn't realize it was this big. I came with only a hundred taels of gold. I can't cover the cost!' His admission was baffling. 'You didn't know its size?' I asked. His reply was even more astonishing: 'I didn't even know it was charcoal!'"

Bian Five paused, waving his hand as if to dispel the tension of the memory. "At that moment, Brother Three nudged me and whispered, 'This is Asim Dingle's son!' I burst out, 'Why did you come?' Isaam Dingle repeated, 'My mother sent me!'"

Fernsby offered a rueful smile. "He kept repeating the same phrase, so I pressed further, 'Didn't your mother tell you about the charcoal's size?' Isaam Dingle shook his head, looking genuinely perplexed. 'No, she didn't. There are many strange aspects to this; even I don't fully understand.'"

Fernsby spread his hands, as if to illustrate his helplessness in the face of the mystery. "His words left me at a loss. The events surrounding his father's dealings with us, his death in the Autumn charcoal kiln, and the absence of his remains were complex. If Isaam Dingle was unaware, it wasn't our place to enlighten him. I simply said, 'I'm sorry, but until you have enough gold, the charcoal remains with us.' He stared at the charcoal, words forming silently on his lips, a strange expression crossing his face."

Bian Five continued, "Given the peculiarity of the situation, I hoped he might say more, shed some light on the enigma. But instead, he stood and remarked, 'Now I know how much gold is needed. My business is growing. Soon, I will return with the required amount.' With that, he left, and the meeting ended."

I jumped in, "Did Isaam Dingle ever return?"

Fernsby shook his head. "No, he never did."

I tried to piece together the puzzle, desperately searching for a thread to weave through the disjointed, bizarre events and individuals that could yield a coherent narrative. But clarity eluded me.

The central figures were the Uncle Four, Asim Dingle, Isaam Dingle, and Asim Dingle's wife—main players in this drama. Supporting them were Aunt Four, Bian Five, and Fernsby.

The facts were sparse but significant: Asim Dingle had initiated the search for a piece of wood and requested to open the kiln. After Uncle Four's return from Whitby, he and Fernsby discovered the charcoal amidst the kiln's ashes. It was as if Uncle Four anticipated someone would seek this charcoal—and indeed, Isaam Dingle had appeared.

Yet, Isaam Dingle was ignorant of the charcoal's importance, merely following his mother's directive. This suggested an unseen hand in these peculiar events—Asim Dingle's wife, Isaam Dingle's mother, whose actions and intentions remained shrouded in mystery.

I pondered this, reaching the conclusion that Asim Dingle's wife was a key player, yet it brought no further insights.

We sat in silence, the room heavy with contemplation, until Fernsby finally spoke. "Our circumstances have deteriorated. We've accrued debts and sold nearly everything. I suggested selling the land and house, but Aunt Four refused. Ultimately, with no options left, we thought of the charcoal again."

I asked, "So you advertised once more, hoping Isaam Dingle might see it and return?"

Fernsby nodded. "Yes, but instead, we were contacted by a scoundrel."

The "scoundrel" was, of course, Harlan.

At that moment, I shared Fernsby's sentiment regarding Harlan. Explaining the charcoal's significance to him would be a monumental task, one that could stretch on indefinitely.

Fernsby continued, "Then Boss Sallow arrived. He spoke with Aunt Four at length. Soon after, you came along."

As Fernsby finished, Bian Five chimed in, "We've shared everything we know about the charcoal with you."

Flora and I exchanged a glance, both of us convinced that they had indeed revealed all they knew, holding back no secrets.

Although Fernsby and Bian Five divulged everything they knew, their knowledge was scarce, leaving us with more questions than answers.

Flora and I rose to leave, exchanging farewells with Fernsby and Bian Five, who graciously saw us to the door. Once seated in the car, I placed the wooden box beside me, its presence a constant reminder of the mystery we were unraveling.

As I drove, my mind churned through the puzzle pieces, trying to fit them together. Flora, equally engrossed in thought, suddenly spoke. "Asim Dingle's wife is a pivotal figure in all of this."

Her insight aligned perfectly with my own. I ventured further, "Your father must be convinced that Isaam Dingle will eventually purchase the charcoal. That's why he urged us to secure it first."

Flora pondered, "But why is he so certain?"

A thought struck me. "Could it be that Isaam Dingle is a prominent figure in the business world, and we're simply unaware?"

Flora nodded thoughtfully. "It's quite possible. We should check the Whitby Celebrity Directory. If Isaam Dingle is listed, we could reach out to him directly."

"I agree," I replied. "I'm eager to learn more about why Uncle Four lingered in Whitby for a month."

"Absolutely," Flora said. "At least Isaam Dingle showed interest in the charcoal, even if he wasn't prepared for the high price."

Once home, I wasted no time heading to the study, pulling out the Celebrity Directory. As I flipped through its pages, I was both startled and embarrassed by what I found.

There, within the directory, was Isaam Dingle's name, occupying a significant section. The entry was laden with accolades and praises, typical of such "celebrity lists." I sifted through the flattery and focused on the essentials, copying Isaam Dingle's biography for Flora, recognizing his crucial role in our unfolding tale.

Isaam Dingle's biography read: "Born in 1940 in Whitby, Yorkshire, Isaam Dingle lost his father early in life.

Post-World War II, he relocated to Brunei with his mother. Industrious and committed to learning, he started as a laborer in a forestry farm. Through diligence, he eventually managed multiple forest farms. By the early 1970s, amidst a global paper industry crisis, he had the foresight to establish a large pulp mill, supplying paper mills worldwide. His business flourished, earning him a reputation as a leading figure in Brunei. Known for his philanthropy and generosity, he is widely revered."

Amazed by the revelation, I called Flora to the study. "Take a look at this," I said, pointing to the biography. "He's a paper industry magnate in Brunei!"

Flora glanced at the publication date of the celebrity directory, noting it was released just a year ago. A frown creased her forehead. "It's peculiar," she mused. "Back then, Isaam Dingle didn't have enough gold to trade for the charcoal. Given his current standing, he should easily have the resources. Why hasn't he reached out to Aunt Four?"

I shrugged, spreading my hands in a gesture of uncertainty. "I'm not sure. There might be another reason. But discovering his identity and his interest in this piece of charcoal is crucial."

Flora smiled knowingly. "So, what's the plan? Are you thinking of traveling to Brunei to pitch the charcoal to him?"

The thought of door-to-door salesmanship made me cringe slightly. Yet, Isaam Dingle's past interest in the charcoal lingered at the edge of my curiosity, hinting at unanswered questions. Meeting him seemed inevitable.

As I wavered, Flora suggested, "Perhaps we should send him a telegram first, gauge his response?"

I agreed, nodding. "That sounds good. I'd be pretty awkward trying to sell it in person anyway."

With that, I pulled out a sheet of paper and drafted a succinct telegram using the office address listed for Isaam Dingle in the directory. The message was straightforward, reminding him of his previous interest in the charcoal, which he hadn't acquired due to its high cost, and letting him know it was now in my possession. If he remained interested, I invited him to contact me.

We sent the telegram that same day, anticipating a reply by the following day or, at the latest, the day after.

Meanwhile, I had another critical task: to scrutinize the charcoal thoroughly.

I retrieved the charcoal, along with an assortment of other charcoal pieces that my butler, Wilson, had procured.

Under a 60x magnifying glass, I meticulously compared the special piece to the ordinary ones, searching for any discernible differences.

Despite an afternoon of painstaking examination, nothing set it apart. I even scraped off some charcoal powder to conduct rudimentary tests with all the equipment at my disposal. The chemical reactions were indistinguishable from those of regular charcoal.

I had speculated that something unique might reside at its core, so I weighed it against its volume, but its weight revealed nothing out of the ordinary.

Breaking the charcoal open to explore its interior was a tempting last resort, yet I refrained. The charcoal's worth—equivalent to its volume in gold—depended on its intact state. Who could say if it would retain value once broken?

After a fruitless afternoon, I found no new insights. That evening, post-dinner, I phoned Flora's father. "I've secured the charcoal from Aunt Four," I informed him.

"Excellent!" he responded enthusiastically.

I chuckled, a touch bemused. "I've examined it with every method I have. It's just a piece of charcoal!"

"Did Aunt Four mention its origins?" Boss Sallow inquired.

"No," I admitted. "But Fernsby and Bian Five shared what they knew, though they didn't understand the why of it."

Boss Sallow mused, "I think Isaam Dingle might hold the key to that mystery."

"I've already reached out to him via telegram," I said eagerly. "If he knows the charcoal's secret, he'll surely contact me."

Boss Sallow laughed heartily. "When he does, make sure you set a sky-high price!"

Unsure how to respond, I murmured a vague agreement. Realizing Boss Sallow knew as little as I did, further conversation seemed futile. We exchanged goodbyes, and I hung up, left to ponder the enigma of the charcoal once more.

The charcoal lay on my desk, an enigma wrapped in shadow. I watched it for a moment longer, then carefully placed it into its exquisite box, took it, and worked out of the study. Flora intercepted me, a knowing smile playing at her lips.

"Be careful," she cautioned, "don't break it!"

"If breaking it leads to answers, then so be it," I replied with a hint of defiance.

Flora's eyes widened. "You're going to—"

"Yes," I interjected, "an X-ray. Let's see what mysteries lie within."

She chuckled softly. "I knew that once this piece of charcoal found its way into your hands, sleep would become a distant memory."

"Are you sleeping well?" I shot back, arching an eyebrow.

Her silence was her answer. As I drove to a friend's studio, my mind raced ahead. My friend, Peter, was an expert in X-ray inspections, particularly of metal structures. His studio was equipped with the latest technology, and I had reached out to him before embarking on this journey.

The car rolled through the factory's formidable iron gates, guided by the attendant toward a nondescript building. Peter awaited me at the entrance, clad in a white lab coat, his expression one of anticipation. His eyes lit up when he saw the ornate box.

"What's in there?" he asked with a playful whistle. "A hidden treasure?"

"Would you believe me if I said it's just a piece of charcoal?" I grinned.

He blinked in disbelief. "You're kidding!"

I laughed, "No joke. I need to see if there's more to it than meets the eye."

Understanding my peculiar curiosity, Peter merely muttered, "What could possibly be in there? Certainly not a diamond!"

I remained silent, clutching the box and a paper bag filled with ordinary charcoal purchased at an ordinary price. Together, we entered the X-ray room, donning white gowns to match the sterile environment. As I extracted the charcoal from its box, Peter's face twisted into an expression of incredulity.

Gently, he placed the charcoal into position, his fingers dancing over controls as he directed my attention to a large screen. The state-of-the-art X-ray machine promised instant results, revealing secrets hidden beneath the surface.

As he dimmed the lights and initiated the scan, an unexpected itch distracted me, drawing my gaze away for just a fraction of a second. Suddenly, Peter's scream shattered the silence—a sound so raw and fear-laden that it cut through the room like a knife.

Before I could grasp what was unfolding, a forceful impact sent me reeling. The blow was so unexpected that I almost toppled over. Regaining my balance, I spun around to find that it was Peter who had collided with me.

He seemed to be backing away rapidly, his movements erratic, as if intoxicated. Despite the jarring collision, I reached out instinctively to steady him. His eyes were wide with terror, his face a mask of dread. It was clear that something extraordinary had occurred.

I scanned the room, but saw nothing out of the ordinary. An eerie silence enveloped us, broken only by Peter's ragged breathing.

"What happened?" I demanded, urgency in my voice.

Still trembling, Peter pointed a quivering finger at the screen. I followed his gesture, my eyes landing on the display. The screen showed a nondescript gray area—the X-ray image of the charcoal.

Confusion gripped me. What about this image could have terrified Peter so thoroughly?

"What's wrong?" I pressed, seeking clarity.

"You—you didn't see it?" he stammered, his voice shaky.

"What did you see?" I asked, bewildered.

Peter blinked rapidly, still fixated on the screen, as if trying to reconcile the vision with reality. After a long pause, he mumbled, "Sorry, I must have been seeing things. If you didn't see it, then I must have imagined it."

"Earlier, I looked away for just a second," I admitted. "Tell me, what did you see?"

Having regained some composure, Peter managed a nervous laugh. "For a moment, I thought I saw a person appear on the screen."

His words left me speechless. A person? On the X-ray screen? This was no ordinary monitor—it revealed the internal structure of the charcoal. If Peter perceived a human figure there, it implied something impossible, something inconceivable.

The notion defied logic; it was beyond comprehension. My mind raced with countless theories about what could be hidden inside the charcoal, yet none included the presence of a person. That was simply unthinkable.

For a moment, I was at a loss, words failing me. I could only stare at Peter, silently urging him to provide some rational explanation for this bizarre occurrence.

CHAPTER 7

A Man in the Charcoal

Peter managed a sheepish smile. "Did I scare you? Look, the X-ray shows nothing unusual inside the charcoal."

"But you said you saw a person," I pressed, my curiosity mingling with frustration.

Peter waved it off. "I must have been seeing things."

I wasn't convinced. "If it was just a trick of the eye, you wouldn't have reacted like that. Did you really see a person?"

Grabbing him by the shoulders, I shook him lightly, trying to jolt some truth from him. He broke free, raising his hands defensively. "Let me explain!"

I released him, and he continued, "The screen might have reflected our shadows. With the lighting and the glass, it could easily play tricks on the eyes."

His explanation seemed plausible, a logical solution to an illogical event. Yet, a seed of doubt lingered in my mind.

"You got so scared just by seeing a figure?" I questioned, probing for more.

Peter offered a wan smile. "I must be overworked."

"Tell me the truth!" I insisted, not willing to let it go.

His face reddened, and he snapped, "Why would I lie? You wanted to see the inside of the charcoal, and now you do! What are you expecting to find—a person trapped inside, trying to escape?"

His last words hung in the air, bizarre yet strangely compelling.

"Is that what you saw?" I asked, trying to piece together the puzzle.

His face flushed deeper, and he confessed with a mix of anger and resignation, "Yes, a person, struggling, trying to get out—but I couldn't hear him."

Despite his agitation, I placed a reassuring hand on his shoulder. "Calm down, you're exhausted. I apologize for causing more stress."

He chuckled ruefully, eager to shift focus. "Do you want the X-ray photos? The machine automatically takes them every ten seconds."

My interest piqued, I quickly asked, "How many have been taken?"

"Thirty-seven," he replied.

"Develop them all," I said, sensing a potential breakthrough.

Peter nodded, switched off the machine, and sent the film for processing. As he did, he hesitated, as if weighing his words. "I hope the photos don't show what I saw."

"Thank you," I said, appreciating his candor.

He opened another box, took out a film box, placed it on a conveyor belt, and sent it out. Pressing a button on the intercom, he said, "Mike, I need these photos immediately!" Then, he turned around and added, "In about ten minutes, you can see those photos!" He then slumped into a chair, visibly drained. As I paced the room, the charcoal still held my fascination. Almost instinctively, I brought it to my ear, listening for something—anything. Of course, there was only silence.

Peter observed my futile gesture. "What's special about this piece of charcoal?"

"I don't know," I replied honestly. "That's what I'm trying to discover."

A voice crackled over the intercom, announcing the photos' arrival. Peter retrieved them, placing them under a lamp for examination.

"Start with the first one," I instructed.

One by one, the images revealed the same gray monotony, no hints of hidden figures or trapped souls. My frustration grew as each photo failed to shed light on the mystery.

"You said the equipment is advanced," I said, grasping at straws. "Does it record video?"

Peter's eyes lit up with realization. "Of course! How could I forget?"

He rushed to the console, flipping open a lid, but his expression quickly morphed from excitement to despair.

Concerned, I hurried over. "What's wrong?"

Peter stepped back, a rueful smile on his lips. "There's no videotape inside, so there's no video," he admitted.

I scrutinized him, sensing there was more beneath the surface. "You wish there was a videotape, don't you?" I asked, probing deeper.

Avoiding my gaze, he deflected, "Me? Don't you wish for one, too?"

His evasiveness confirmed my suspicion. "No, you want it more than I do. You want evidence that you weren't imagining things, proof that you really saw someone on that screen."

His complexion turned ashen, and he nodded reluctantly. "Yes—yes."

I placed a steadying hand on his shoulder, feeling the tremor coursing through him. "Tell me what you saw, Peter."

He looked at me, eyes pleading for understanding, but I held my ground. Finally, he relented with a heavy sigh. "I really saw a person," he confessed.

He gestured toward the screen. "As soon as the X-ray machine powered on, there he was—reaching out, waving, as if trying to get my attention."

I inhaled sharply. "You saw it so clearly? What did they look like?"

His smile was a pained grimace. "I can't say for sure. It was more of a shadow, a blur, but the impression was so strong—I just knew it was a person."

Though his description was vague, his sincerity was unmistakable. "And then?"

"Then," he continued bitterly, "I panicked. I screamed, stumbled back, and ran into you."

I recalled the incident, the screen's gray void that followed his outburst. "It only lasted a moment?"

Peter nodded, his face drained of color. "A second, maybe less."

"Let's try again," I suggested, eager to unravel the mystery.

With a nod, he repositioned the charcoal and gestured for me to watch the screen. This time, I vowed to keep my eyes glued to it, no matter what. But when he activated the machine, only the familiar gray expanse greeted us—no phantom figure in sight.

Peter's shoulders slumped, and I sighed, asking him for the photos from earlier. "Of course," he replied wearily.

I walked towards the stack of photos and organized them sequentially. While arranging them, I suddenly noticed several messy and irregular lines in the first photo. I had seen this photo on a milky white glowing glass plate before, but at that time, I was focused on finding a person in the photo and overlooked the delicate lines. It was only then that I noticed them.

Under the milky white backlight, they stood out more sharply.

"Peter, take a look at this," I called, pointing to the lines.

He examined them closely. "Could be a scratch from the development process," he mused.

I shook my head. "No, these are waveforms."

He leaned in, scrutinizing the patterns. "It does resemble waveforms, but X-ray machines don't capture sound or waveforms."

"The machine itself can't," I agreed, "but the screen's display structure might inadvertently capture waveforms."

Peter considered this. "It's theoretically possible, but such patterns should be random. These seem too orderly."

His remark intrigued me. What appeared chaotic to me seemed structured to him. "Orderly? How so?"

He explained, "These waveforms resemble sound waves, like those from a wooden flute."

Confusion flooded my mind, unable to grasp the implications. Peter, noting my bewilderment, elaborated, "Different sounds produce unique waveforms. A scream, a speech, a violin note—each has its own pattern."

"I see," I nodded. "So, you think these resemble flute sounds?"

"Not exactly," he clarified. "They just remind me of them. And if they are sound waves, their frequency is incredibly high—over 30,000 Hz."

I was taken aback. "That's beyond human hearing!"

"Exactly," he said. "If these are sound waves, we can't hear them."

He paused, reflecting. "Did we hear anything earlier?"

I said, "No, except for your scream."

Peter replied, "My scream has a frequency of about 17,000 Hz. If displayed, the waveform is not sharp but rather flat. If this set is a waveform, I think it may be caused by the mechanical device when the X-ray machine starts to operate."

I was full of doubts and didn't know what to say. After a long pause, I asked, "Peter, you just said that different sounds have different waveforms?"

"Yes!" Peter confirmed.

I continued, "Then, in theory, as long as you see different waveforms, you can restore it and know what sound it is?"

"In theory, but in practice, there is no instrument to restore waveforms accurately," Peter explained. "No one can identify what sound it is based on the waveform alone because many sounds that seem very different to us look similar in their waveforms. Especially when it is not a single tone, it is even more difficult to distinguish."

I stared at the set of waveforms in the photo, wanting to say something but stopping myself. Peter then asked, "Have you heard the joke among my friends?"

In that situation, I had no mood for jokes, but I nodded. Peter continued, "There's a music lover who boasts he can recognize any music just by looking at its waveform without using his ears. He made a bet and, while staring at the changing waveform on the screen, confidently declared it was Beethoven's 'Pastoral Symphony.' It turned out to be the first movement of Rossini's 'William Tell Overture.'"

Peter called it a joke, but I didn't find it funny.

Not only did I not find it funny, but I also thought that this person was quite impressive. The first movement of the "William Tell Overture" is about the pastoral scenery of Switzerland and has a similar waveform to the Pastoral Symphony, which isn't surprising!

I sighed and pointed at the photo, saying, "If this set of waveforms is caused by sound, you mean no one can tell what the sound is?"

Peter said, "I don't think so. Besides, it's useless to identify it because this is a sound that human ears cannot hear."

I nodded thoughtfully, digesting Peter's explanation. The idea that these waveforms could represent an inaudible sound intrigued me, though it did little to clarify the mystery.

"So," I mused, "even if we could identify the sound, it wouldn't matter because it's beyond our hearing range?"

"Exactly," Peter confirmed. "It's like trying to describe a color that doesn't exist in the visible spectrum."

The analogy resonated with me, highlighting the futility of our situation. We were dealing with phenomena at the fringes of our understanding, where conventional logic offered little guidance.

I glanced again at the photo, the waveforms an enigma etched in lines and curves. "And there's no technology to convert these into something we can understand?"

"Not reliably," he admitted. "Sound wave interpretation is a complex field, and even slight variations can lead to vastly different interpretations."

Though his words were sobering, they also stirred a sense of wonder. What if this charcoal held secrets that defied our current comprehension? What if the waveforms were a message or signal from an unknown source, waiting to be decoded?

Peter's joke about the music lover lingered in my mind. It was a reminder of the limitations of human perception, and how easily we can be led astray by our senses.

But I couldn't shake the feeling that there was more to this than met the eye—or the ear. The image of a person trapped within the charcoal, though seemingly impossible, hinted at something extraordinary.

As I left Peter's lab, the photograph tucked safely in my pocket, I resolved to delve deeper. Perhaps the answers lay not in what we could hear or see, but in embracing the unknown and daring to explore its mysteries.

Back home, Flora awaited me, her expression a mix of curiosity and concern. I recounted the day's events, and she questioned why I hadn't kept my eyes glued to the screen. Her words only exacerbated my regret—I had missed a crucial moment.

"I just looked away for a second," I lamented, striking my head in frustration.

Flora's frown deepened as she mulled over the strange events. "Peter's claim is puzzling," I admitted. "If he really saw a person on the X-ray screen, logically, that person would have to be inside the charcoal."

I tapped the box containing the enigmatic piece of charcoal for emphasis. Flora pondered this, her analytical mind at work. "The X-ray shows the internal structure, right?"

"Exactly," I confirmed.

"So, seeing a person is illogical," Flora said, waving her hand dismissively. "If there were a person, they'd appear as a skeleton."

Her insight left me momentarily speechless. It was a perspective I hadn't considered. If a person were truly inside the charcoal, the X-ray would reveal only bones.

I sought her opinion, eager for clarity. "What's your explanation?"

Flora chose her words carefully. "Perhaps it was just a shadow. The variations in gray shades could create an illusion, making it seem like a person was there."

I nodded slowly. "It makes sense, but why did the shadow vanish?"

"Maybe the screen's cathode tube wasn't properly calibrated, or the X-ray machine's initial power was too low, resulting in a transient image," she suggested.

Her logic was sound, yet something about it left me restless. Flora chuckled, attempting to lighten the mood.

"Despite all the strange things we've experienced, a person trapped inside charcoal defies all logic."

I couldn't argue with her reasoning, but it didn't quench my curiosity. "There are many unexplainable phenomena in this world," I murmured. "They exist, even if they defy explanation."

Flora chose not to debate further. "Let's sleep on it. Once Isaam Dingle responds, we might have more answers."

Her suggestion was sensible, but it didn't ease the knot of questions in my mind. I reluctantly placed the wooden box in a cabinet. Before closing it, I couldn't resist one last glare at the charcoal, as if challenging it to reveal its secrets.

With a resigned sigh, I turned away, knowing that for now, all I could do was wait.

That night, my sleep was haunted by an unsettling dream. I found myself inside a piece of charcoal, a place that defied logic and reason. In waking moments, I would dismiss the notion of "a person in charcoal" as impossible—charcoal is solid, impenetrable. Yet, in the dream, it was as though the charcoal had transformed into a room, confining yet accommodating my every move. The solid walls did not impede me; they seemed to breathe and shift as I did.

Awaking from such a fantastical dream left me with a lingering sense of wonder, as if the impossible were teasing the edges of reality. The dream's absurdity was undeniable, but its resonance stayed with me, as if foretelling something extraordinary.

The following day, anticipation gnawed at me as I awaited Isaam Ding;e's response. The hours dragged into evening with no word, leaving me restless and impatient. Over dinner, I voiced my frustration to Flora. "Do you think Brunei is too remote for telegrams to reach us?"

She gave me a reproachful look. "It's not that backward."

Her answer did little to settle my nerves, and I found myself pushing away my plate, appetite gone. Then, as if on cue, the doorbell chimed. I sprang up, my heart leaping at the sound of that long-awaited word: telegram!

It was from Isaam Dingle.

The message was succinct, almost cryptic, and not what I had expected:

"Mr. Morris: I received your message. Please forgive me for being too busy with worldly affairs and unable to meet you. But I hope you can come to Brunei for a chat, Isaam Dingle."

The brevity of the telegram left me pondering its implications. An invitation to Brunei was unexpected.

After reading the first telegram, both Flora and I were left in a state of perplexed silence. The indifference in Isaam Dingle's response was unexpected, especially given the mysterious nature of the charcoal. Isaam Dingle's previous willingness to trade it for gold suggested its significance, yet his telegram showed no urgency or keen interest.

I felt unsettled by his apparent lack of concern. Flora, sensing my frustration, asked, "What are you going to do?"

I shook my head, smiling bitterly. "It seems like he's not interested at all."

"Not necessarily," Flora countered. "He did invite you to Brunei, so there must be some interest."

Her point was valid, but I remained skeptical. "But this charcoal is tied to his father's peculiar actions and death, and he didn't even mention it."

Flora pondered this, trying to make sense of his reaction. "Maybe Isaam Dingle truly knows nothing about it. Remember, he said it was his mother who sent him when he first encountered Fernsby and Bian Five."

Frustrated, I threw the telegram to the floor. "Forget it. I'm done with this."

The disappointment of waiting two days for such a lukewarm response was palpable. I entertained the idea of burning the charcoal someday, envisioning the warmth it could provide as a form of luxurious irony.

Yet, less than two hours later, the situation shifted dramatically. Flora began packing my bags, as I prepared to head to Brunei the next morning.

The catalyst was Isaam Dingle's second telegram, which arrived unexpectedly soon after the first. It read, "Mr. Morris: Regarding the charcoal, I talked to my mother. She urged me to accompany her to meet you immediately. However, my mother is old and weak and cannot move. Please come to Brunei as soon as possible. Please forgive me if you have to. Isaam Dingle."

This second message validated Flora's earlier guess. Isaam Dingle himself might have been ignorant of the charcoal's significance, but his mother, the widow of Asim Dingle, held the key. The first telegram was likely a casual reply, sent before he consulted her. Upon learning the details, she understood the urgency and insisted on seeing me.

It became clear that Isaam Dingle's mother, the woman behind the strange behaviors of the past, was the true linchpin in this mystery. With renewed determination, I prepared to uncover the secrets that lay ahead in Brunei, convinced that answers awaited in the form of an elderly lady with knowledge of the charcoal's enigmatic past.

The excitement of the unfolding mystery kept me awake that night. Flora and I speculated endlessly about Mrs. Dingle's interest in the charcoal and what secrets she might hold. Our discussions circled around possibilities but yielded no concrete conclusions. Meanwhile, I took the opportunity to learn the distinct dialect of Whitby from a friend.

The complexity of British dialects is astounding, each with its unique nuances and sounds. Though London isn't known for particularly complex dialects, the regions around Yorkshire, including Sheffield, boast unique linguistic traits. My intent was clear: if Mrs. Dingle had a lingering nostalgia for her hometown, speaking in her native dialect might elicit more information from her.

After a sleepless night of linguistic practice, I set off, navigating travel formalities before boarding my flight. The plane ride offered some much-needed rest, and soon I found myself stepping off at Brunei's airport.

Traveling light, I quickly spotted a local holding a sign with my name. Beside him stood a frail-looking man—not the image of a thriving businessman. As I approached, he extended his hand warmly. "Mr. Morris? I'm Isaam Dingle."

Flora had informed him of my arrival, so he awaited me at the airport. He eyed my suitcase, prompting me to clarify, "Mr. Dingle, the charcoal is in here."

"Please, my car is outside," he replied, motioning for his assistant to take my luggage.

Isaam Dingle's apparent success was reflected in his luxurious car and uniformed driver. As we drove, I sensed his hesitation to broach certain topics. I offered encouragement, "Feel free to speak your mind."

He hesitated, then confessed, "Exchanging a piece of charcoal for gold seems absurd."

"Is that why you distanced yourself after seeing it years ago?" I probed.

"You could say that," he admitted. "I left UK at four. Brunei is home, and the charcoal ties to a past I have no interest in."

I nodded, understanding his detachment from the past. "I see."

Isaam Dingle continued, "But my mother cherishes those memories. Mr. Morris, forgive my directness, but if you're hoping to exploit her nostalgia for personal gain, you'll fail."

His bluntness tested my patience, but I let him finish. His self-assured expression begged a response, so I replied coolly, "Mr. Dingle, rest assured, if I sought monetary gain, small businessmen like yourself wouldn't be my focus."

CHAPTER 8

The Secret Room in
the Ancestral Mansion

The air was thick with tension as Isaam Dingle arched an eyebrow. "Really? And who, exactly, is your target?"

I leaned back, a sly smile playing on my lips. "Spring Miracle, for instance. Now, he's quite impressive."

Spring Miracle was not just any wealthy individual. He was the kind of man who, upon receiving my call, promptly dispatched a check for five million dollars. Unlike Isaam Dingle, a modestly successful businessman, Miracle was a magnate in every sense of the word. I dropped his name not merely because I knew him, but because he, too, was in Brunei, an esteemed guest of the King himself.

The mention of Miracle's name hit Isaam Dingle like a physical blow, leaving him reeling.

"And I hear Mr. Miracle has extensive ventures and oil fields in Brunei," I continued, a hint of challenge in my voice. "Surely, Mr. Dingle, your business empire rivals his?"

Isaam Dingle's face twisted in discomfort, words failing him until he managed to stammer, "Mr. Morris, do... do you know Mr. Miracle?"

I chuckled lightly. "I wouldn't claim to know him well, but we've met. Enough that he wouldn't suspect me of deceit."

Isaam Dingle's expression soured further, a mix of embarrassment and frustration. After a pause, he muttered, "I'm merely looking out for myself. No offense intended."

I merely hummed in response, uninterested in further conversation. We drove on in silence, the car winding through the lush Brunei landscape until we arrived at an expansive villa. The vehicle rolled to a stop in front of the grand entrance.

As Isaam Dingle and I stepped out of the car, the humid air of Brunei enveloped us. A native aide dutifully carried my box as we approached the villa, where we were immediately greeted by the echo of an eager voice. "Isaam, is Mr. Morris here?" Her accent was unmistakably Whitby.

Recognizing the call, I responded with the same Whitby accent, "He's here!"

A ripple of excitement followed, and I turned to see a maid carefully guiding a wheelchair forward. Seated within was an elderly lady, her eyes bright with anticipation. She seemed to be in her early sixties, her face a tapestry of warmth and eagerness as she scanned the room, searching for the source of the voice that had answered her.

Wasting no time, I approached her with a friendly smile. "Mrs. Dingle? I'm Ash Morris!" I announced, ready to unravel the layers of intrigue that seemed to surround this meeting.

Her grip was surprisingly firm as she clasped my hands, her lips quivering with emotion. Isaam Dingle trailed behind, and I couldn't resist a teasing remark. "Given your mother's reaction, one might think swindling you will be as easy as a piece of cake."

Isaam Dingle flushed, visibly perturbed, but remained silent.

Mrs. Dingle's breathing was labored as she finally spoke. "Mr. Morris, where is that thing? Did you bring it?"

Her words caught me off guard. "That thing" referred, of course, to the charcoal. Yet, her choice of words puzzled me.

Why not call it what it was? My hesitation only seemed to agitate her further.

"I brought it," I assured her quickly.

Hearing this, Mrs. Dingle visibly relaxed, casting a knowing glance at her son. "Isaam once mentioned... a piece of charcoal?"

I was puzzled, the mystery deepening. Mrs. Dingle wasn't aware of the charcoal's true nature, much like Uncle Four's obliviousness when he retrieved it from the Autumn kiln. Why the secrecy?

As I pondered, Mrs. Dingle's urgency returned. "Give it to me! The charcoal!"

Her desperation was palpable, and she struggled to rise, alarming both her nurse and Isaam Dingle, who quickly intervened.

"Mother!" Isaam Dingle pleaded, his voice tight with anxiety.

Ignoring him, Mrs. Dingle insisted, "Pay him, Isaam. Whatever he demands, pay it!"

Isaam Dingle's face was a storm of conflicting emotions, yet he dared not defy her.

Caught in the unfolding drama, I felt a twinge of unease. If I named a price now, it might confirm Isaam Dingle's suspicions of deceit.

Isaam Dingle murmured softly, "Mother, there's something I must tell you."

Her response was fierce. "No more words. You don't understand. Whatever the cost, even if it means losing everything, I must have it!"

Her conviction was startling, and in that moment, I was certain Mrs. Dingle knew the true value of the charcoal. Her resolve was unwavering, and the air crackled with the weight of unspoken truths.

Seeing Isaam Dingle's discomfort brought a subtle satisfaction, a small victory after his earlier rudeness. But I couldn't afford to dwell on it; I needed the information Mrs. Dingle held.

"Mrs. Dingle," I began, trying to ease the tension, "let's not worry about the price just yet. Here, let me give you this piece of charcoal first."

With careful hands, I opened my suitcase and retrieved the charcoal box, presenting it to her. She clutched it tightly, her eyes locked onto the piece within, her face a canvas of overwhelming emotion. It was perplexing—what could a simple piece of charcoal mean to her?

After a moment, she wiped her tears and looked up, her voice steady yet urgent. "Mr. Morris, please come with me. There's so much I need to tell you, so much."

The emphasis in her words was clear, and I nodded, eager for answers. "I have much to say as well," I replied, the anticipation palpable.

Mrs. Dingle took a breath, her gaze shifting to her son. "Isaam, you should join us."

But Isaam Dingle shook his head, his tone dismissive. "I'm busy. I don't need to hear about the past. I have my own matters to attend to."

Mrs. Dingle studied him, a sigh escaping her lips. "Very well. If you choose not to listen, that's your decision. Mr. Morris, follow me."

She indicated for the nurse to wheel her upstairs. As they moved, I turned to Isaam. "Mr. Dingle, you might reconsider. This concerns your father deeply."

His response was cold, unwavering. "My father has been gone for years. Whatever concerns him, I'm not interested."

His resolve was formidable, and I realized persuasion would be futile. I followed Mrs. Dingle upstairs, her wheelchair gliding into a spacious room, then out onto a balcony adorned with flowers. The view stretched over a serene garden, framed by distant hills.

Settling into a rattan chair opposite Mrs. Dingle, we were joined by a servant who brought tea. The tranquility of the setting belied the weight of the conversation to come.

Mrs. Dingle clutched the charcoal, lost in thought. I waited patiently, sensing the story she was about to unravel was significant.

"My family has always valued education," she began, her voice reflective. "I was fortunate to attend school and later taught at a primary school in my hometown. Mr. Dingle was the principal there."

Her narrative unfolded, and I leaned in, listening intently.

"Mr. Dingle's family lived west of the county," she continued. "The area was known as 'Long Meadow Camp.' It was settled by people not originally from the village."

The name intrigued me, and I asked, "Why is it called that?"

"Long Meadow Camp," she explained, "was home to people once referred to as 'Long Meadow.'"

The term struck a chord. "Ah," I murmured, recalling its historical significance. "Long Meadow refers to the area where the Luddites had their encampments, doesn't it?"

Mrs. Dingle nodded, her expression solemn. "Yes, they were descendants of the Luddites. When the government forces cracked down, these people fled, some settling in our county."

I nodded in understanding, though a part of me grew impatient. Her tale seemed to wade through history, yet I yearned for the crux of our meeting. Gently, I prodded, "Back then, Mr. Dingle did something quite unusual. He went to a place where charcoal was burned—"

The air felt charged with the promise of revelations, and I hoped her next words would illuminate the mystery at hand.

Old Lady Dingle waved her hand, cutting off my impatience. "Don't rush. To understand, you must start from the beginning."

I offered a resigned smile. I was here, after all, and if she preferred to begin at the outset, so be it.

She continued, "These Luddites were officials, some even high-ranking, rumored to be crowned as kings!"

I nodded, acknowledging the historical context. "Indeed, in the later years of the Luddite Rebellion, it was not uncommon to see many leaders wandering the streets."

Old Lady Dingle's smile turned wistful. "I never knew if Asim's ancestors were leaders or what their status was. I was a schoolteacher, he the principal. Within a year, our relationship blossomed, and we spoke of marriage."

Her face softened with the memory, and I let her story unfold. Though ordinary, it was a window into her past, one I hoped would soon reveal its significance.

"My family opposed our marriage," she continued, "but I was determined to marry Asim, and they eventually consented. I moved into his home—his parents had long passed. It was a grand house, three entrances, built with solid water-ground blue bricks."

She paused, a hint of pride in her voice. "Only two old servants remained, and the house felt vast and empty with just us. So many rooms, places I never dared explore. A year after our marriage, Isaam was born. I stopped teaching. When Asim was three, one night, he was asleep when we heard shouting: 'Fire! Fire!'"

Her words quickened, and despite my earlier impatience, I leaned in slightly. "Isaam woke first, crying, and

Asim sprang from bed, rushing outside. I held Isamm close, paralyzed, as the commotion grew."

I stifled a yawn but made sure to listen, sensing the narrative's importance.

"The chaos continued until dawn," she said, her voice steady. "An old servant ran back and forth, reporting the fire's progress. It started on the street behind us. By morning, it was extinguished. The house where it began was reduced to ashes. Only a corner of ours was singed."

She paused, a deep sigh escaping her lips.

I hoped for a shift in the tale, something more than this recollection of domestic life, when she suddenly added, "If only the fire had consumed our house as well."

Her words caught my attention, a revelation wrapped in regret. What seemed a mundane incident was, in fact, intertwined with her fate—and by extension, with Asim Dingle's, and perhaps at the heart of everything I sought to understand.

"At dawn, holding young Isaam, I ventured to the site of destruction—the last section of the house, where a small patio lay behind a once-imposing wall now crumbled. Asim was there already, sleeves rolled up, orchestrating the servants as they cleared the debris. He paused, gesturing for me to come closer, his voice tinged with nostalgia. "Darling, look at this. I used to play here as a child. This house... there's something peculiar about it."

Intrigued, I listened intently as Mrs. Dingle recounted the tale. She, too, was puzzled at Asim's insistence. "He pointed to the wall," she explained. "Built with heavy water-ground blue bricks, it was hollow, two layers with a gap in between. I thought nothing of it, but he urged me to listen."

"What?" I interjected, surprised. "He asked you to 'listen'?"

"Yes," she nodded, "and then he dropped half a brick down the gap. The sound that followed was not what you'd expect—a hollow echo, suggesting a void beneath, maybe ten feet deep. I gasped, realizing the emptiness below. 'Keep quiet,' Asim had cautioned, eyes darting to the street where neighbors mourned their losses. His caution was clear. "

"There's a cellar under this house," Mrs. Dingle explained, her voice barely a whisper. "Asim had no idea it existed. If not for the fire, it would have remained hidden."

I nodded, piecing together the implications. "A secret cellar in an old house often means hidden treasures, especially given your ancestral connections."

Mrs. Dingle sighed, a bitter smile on her lips. "Treasure," she echoed. "Asim was convinced of it. He spoke of his ancestors with a fervor I hadn't seen before. 'You know what they did,' he said, eyes alight with excitement."

I understood, recalling the Luddites' notorious raids. "Yes, they looted extensively, especially in the affluent regions."

"Exactly," she agreed. "Asim imagined untold wealth lay beneath our feet. 'Think about it,' he urged me, 'there must be something hidden.' His enthusiasm was infectious, yet I couldn't shake a growing dread."

She paused, her face shadowed by regret. "Normally, he would have been angry at my skepticism, but that day, he was too excited. 'You know what the Luddites were capable of,' he kept saying. But as night fell, his excitement turned to restlessness."

I interjected, "So he planned to explore the cellar—"

Mrs. Dingle shot me a look, silencing my interruption. I gestured for her to continue.

"That night, he lit a lantern, urging me to join him. But I was seized by an overwhelming premonition of doom, my fear so intense I trembled. Asim, noticing my distress, had brushed it aside. 'What's the matter?' he asked. 'Don't go,' I implored, 'seal it up instead!'"

"My plea was met with laughter, a sound I could not forget. He reassured me, 'What are you afraid of? Even if there were monsters, they've long since fled.' Yet, his determination was unshakable, and with the lantern in hand, he moved to uncover the cellar's entrance."

Mrs. Dingle stopped, her sorrow palpable. Whatever Asim had found in that cellar, it had led to tragedy—a final journey from which he never returned. I offered words of comfort, "Even had you insisted, it might not have deterred him."

She looked at me, resignation in her eyes. "True. Curiosity is a powerful force. Even I, afraid as I was, wanted to know what lay below."

I nodded, hoping to ease her burden. "Then there's no need for regret."

"Yes," she sighed, "but when he descended, I felt as if we were saying goodbye forever."

I spread my hands, bewildered. "Why such finality over a simple exploration?"

Mrs. Dingle's voice was steady. "I just knew something terrible awaited."

Understanding the inexplicable nature of premonition, I let the silence stretch. She continued, "Asim wiped my tears, promising, 'Nothing will happen.' Then, with the lantern's glow, he disappeared into the darkness below."

Her tale lingered in the air, an echo of choices and destiny, leaving me with the haunting sense that the past was not yet done revealing its secrets.

The air was thick with anticipation as Mrs. Dingle's voice quivered with each word. "I rushed forward and peered through the narrow gap. By daylight, I had noticed it, but the darkness below was impenetrable. Asim, lantern in hand, had already descended, illuminating the corridor that stretched from the crevice into the hidden depths. As he moved further away, swallowed by the shadows, only the faint glimmer of his light remained. I called out, 'Asim, where are you?' His voice echoed back, 'There's a door here!' Then came the heavy thud of something striking against wood. My heart pounded, a drumbeat of dread."

Mrs. Dingle glanced at me, her eyes wide with remembered fear. I could only manage a tight smile, knowing all too well the pull of the unknown.

She continued, "A thunderous crash followed by Asim's triumphant shout, 'The door's open!' I yelled, 'What do you see?' But my words seemed lost in the abyss, swallowed whole by the silence."

"In that moment, how could you resist going down yourself?" I interjected, caught up in the whirlwind of her tale.

Mrs. Dingle nodded, "Had it not been for the children needing me, I would have ventured below without a second thought."

I listened, knowing well the weight of family that held her back. She resumed, "Just as another cry was on my lips, I caught sight of flickering lights and moving shadows. Asim emerged, an iron box clutched in one hand, the lantern in the other. His excitement was palpable. 'Look!' he cried, 'A treasure! A small iron box!' He stood at the base of the gap, tossing the box up to me. It took several attempts before I finally grasped it. It felt light, yet filled with promise. Asim scrambled up, breathless with anticipation."

"As he climbed, he said, 'Inside, there's a small cellar, lined with hemp stone. Only this box was there. We've struck it rich!' I weighed the box in my hands, skeptical. 'It's too light for gold or silver!' I said. Asim laughed, 'There are treasures beyond gold and silver!' He took the box from me, and we hurried inside. In the house, our child Isaam's cries pierced the air. I picked him up, while Asim set the box down, eager to pry it open."

"The lock succumbed to his efforts, and he turned to me with a grin, 'Brace yourself for the treasure's brilliance!' I urged him on, 'Open it!' With a flourish, he lifted the lid. We leaned in, eyes wide, only to be met with the unexpected."

Mrs. Dingle paused, the air tense with mystery. Yet her pause was fleeting. "Inside lay a stack of papers, neatly bound with thread. It resembled an account book."

My curiosity piqued, I asked, "Could there be something of importance written?"

Mrs. Dingle shook her head, deflated. "I don't know."

Surprised, I pressed, "You don't know? What do you mean? There were no words?"

"There were a few lines," she admitted. "The handwriting was meticulous: 'If the descendants of the Dingle family find this book, it is hard to predict whether it will be a disaster or a blessing. It is only for Dingle family eyes. Others, even wives and daughters, must not read it, lest our ancestors find no peace.' Those words made me laugh and fume at once. I handed Isaam to Asim, declaring, 'Your ancestors' rules, your problem!' With that, I stormed out."

The bitter smile played on my lips as Mrs. Dingle's words hung in the air. She spoke of a time when women were mere shadows in the eyes of society, even their own families viewing them as outsiders. Yet, Mrs. Dingle was different. Educated and fiercely independent, she had defied her family's wishes to marry Asim Dingle, embracing a life that was her own. One could only imagine her disdain for such "ancestral words" that shackled her to traditions she loathed.

But what secrets lay within the booklet, sealed away in a small iron box in the hidden cellar? I asked, "You never read what was written in the book?"

Mrs. Dingle shook her head. "No, I stormed out, hoping Asim would follow. But he didn't. Frustration boiled over, so I peeked through the window, though it was veiled with cotton paper. His shadow danced across it, absorbed in the pages of that cursed book."

"Did he ever speak of it?"

"No," she replied, a curious edge in her voice. "After seeing the first page, I never wanted to speak of it again, and neither did he. Yet that night, Isaam's cries pierced the silence. No one tended to him. I rushed inside to find my child wailing, his face swollen, while Asim sat there, lost in thought."

Her recounting was vivid, yet she missed the crux. "Was he still reading the book then?"

Mrs. Dingle frowned. "I calmed Isaam, then turned to Asim, still as stone. I shouted, 'What are you doing?' He startled, muttering, 'Nothing—nothing!' I knew then he hid something. I thought of that first page and sneered, 'What did you see?'"

"Asim's smile was tinged with bitterness as he spoke, 'Don't blame me. Our ancestral instructions forbid us from sharing this with outsiders.' His words only fueled my anger. I scoffed and turned away, choosing to ignore him entirely. The booklet and the small iron box had vanished, hidden away from prying eyes. I had no desire to uncover the Dingle family secrets. What good ever came from being Luddites? Such affiliations often led to tales of murder and arson, acts of shame cloaked in silence."

Years have passed, but Mrs. Dingle's anger still remained palpable. She continued, "We never spoke of it again, as if it never happened. But days later, Asim came home unexpectedly from school. He announced, 'I asked for leave. The dean will manage things.' I was stunned. 'What are you planning?' I demanded. 'I'm going to Harrogate, Yorkshire.' he answered, avoiding my gaze."

"'What business do you have there?' I pressed. But he hesitated, his honesty betraying him. 'Can't let outsiders know?' I mocked. He nodded, defeated. Furious, I declared, 'You go alone. Isaam stays.' 'I was only taking myself,' he assured, packing lightly. 'I'll be back soon,' he promised."

Tears welled in Mrs. Dingle's eyes, her voice cracking with an unshed sob. "But he never returned."

Her sorrow was a living thing, palpable in the room. Asim Dingle's departure left a chasm that words could not bridge. I could only sit in silence, sharing her sighs, as the weight of the unsolved mystery loomed larger than life.

I nodded, acknowledging her pain. "I know," I said softly.

I had intended to reveal the truth about Asim Dingle's accident to her, but uncertainty held my tongue. I wasn't sure what Uncle Four had shared with her, and I feared that the truth might bring fresh sorrow. So, I kept silent.

Mrs. Dingle slowly regained her composure and continued, "After he left, I waited each day for his return. He never mentioned how long he would be gone. Days stretched into endless anticipation, yet Asim did not come back. Then, one afternoon, a stranger appeared at our door. As soon as he saw me, he asked, 'Are you Mrs. Dingle?'"

Her voice wavered, and I could sense the tension of that moment. The stranger's arrival was unexpected and unnerving, casting a shadow over her heart that she could not yet understand.

" Instinctively, I felt a chill. My heart raced, and words failed me. The stranger introduced himself, "My name is Oliver Villin, from Yorkshire."

The moment Mrs. Dingle mentioned this unexpected visitor, I realized he was the Uncle Four. Though I knew his surname was Villin, hearing his full name, Oliver Villin, was new to me.

Mrs. Dingle continued, "When I heard he was from Yorkshire, my heart thudded loudly. I was speechless. Then he delivered the news that shattered my world: 'Mrs. Dingle, I have some unfortunate news. Mr. Asim Dingle is dead.' His words struck like a thunderclap, and everything went dark as I collapsed."

"When I awoke, Mr. Villin was in the living room, seated calmly amid the chaos, as two old servants scurried about in distress. Their frantic cries echoed, "What should we do? What should we do?" But Mr. Villin remained composed, asking, "Does Mr. Dingle have any relatives? Fetch them immediately!"

"Before the servants could respond, I forced myself upright, declaring, 'No, Asim has no relatives. He was the only son, without even distant cousins.' As I began to speak, Mr. Villin's gaze met mine, but my mind was consumed by a single, harrowing thought: Asim is dead. The finality of it echoed in my mind—Asim is dead, and I will never see him again."

Mrs. Dingle's voice faltered, a gasp escaping her lips as she relived the moment. I watched her, my heart heavy with sympathy. She had been so young then, with a toddler barely three years old, and her husband gone without explanation. The blow dealt to such a promising family was unimaginable, and the depth of her grief was profound. Even with the passage of time, the shadow of that loss lingered, a testament to the enduring pain that such tragedies leave in their wake.

CHAPTER 9

Booklet is the Key

Mrs. Dingle took a deep breath, sighed, and continued, "When Mr. Villin heard me say that, he clasped his hands sorrowfully and asked, 'Mrs. Dingle, you don't have children?' His question jolted me back to reality, and I remembered Isaam. I rushed to say, 'Where is Isaam? Find him!' In that moment, all I wanted was to hold my son close."

"Isaam was outside, playing with the other children. An old servant dashed out at my behest to retrieve him," Mrs. Dingle recounted. "Then Mr. Villin approached me and revealed, 'Mrs. Dingle, I am the leader of the Charcoal Gang.' I was taken aback. I had never heard of such a group, and his words made little sense to me. He continued, 'Your husband came to me with a peculiar request that I couldn't accept. What he asked was simple yet unfathomable. He— he actually—"

Mrs. Dingle's face clouded with sorrow. After a moment's pause, she continued, "Mr. Villin then recounted the circumstances of Asim's death, which were so horrific I can hardly bear to repeat them—"

I quickly interjected, "You don't have to. I know all about Mr. Dingle's accident."

Mrs. Dingle regarded me thoughtfully. "For years, I have struggled to believe Mr. Villin's account. He said—he said Asim was burned to death in a charcoal kiln?"

I nodded. "Yes, that's what I know."

Mrs. Dingle fell silent, her voice tinged with bitterness. "Burned to death?"

I rushed to explain, "Mrs. Dingle, it may not have been as you fear. Once the fire started in the charcoal kiln, it was so intense that he likely died instantly, without suffering."

Her eyes widened in shock. She grasped my wrist, "What? Are you saying the fire started after he went inside the kiln?"

Regretting my hasty words, I realized I might have revealed more than intended—perhaps a detail the Uncle Four had omitted. I tried to cover, "I'm not entirely sure. But Mr. Dingle did perish in the kiln. Someone skilled attempted to rescue him and was gravely burned in the process."

Mrs. Dingle absorbed this, her expression dazed. "Mr. Villin was kind enough to console me, despite my grief. He then said, 'I came in haste and didn't bring much cash, but I brought gold. You and your son will be secure.' He placed a heavy cloth bag on the table, spilling out hundreds of taels of gold."

"I protested, 'I don't know you. How can I accept such a gift?' Mr. Villin insisted, 'Consider it a token from me.' Suspicion flared in me, 'Did you kill Asim?' His demeanor shifted, 'I told you how he died!' I accused, 'You must feel guilty, why else be so generous?' Mr. Villin sighed deeply, 'Yes, guilt weighs on me. Mr. Dingle's death is partly my doing. Yet, I cannot fathom why he made such a strange request. He seemed intimately familiar with our local terrain. Was he from around there?'"

"'No,' I replied, 'he only ever left home to study in York!' Mr. Villin pondered, 'Strange. Before we met, he navigated a path known only to woodcutters, leading to a secluded valley called Ashfield.' I interrupted, 'These details mean nothing to me. I don't understand why he left at all. He never confided in me!'"

"Mr. Villin was taken aback by my ignorance, exclaiming, 'You don't know?' I admitted, 'I don't know.' Despite my confusion, I felt an inexplicable trust in him," Mrs. Dingle recounted.

"Perhaps it was his generosity—the gold he offered seemed earnest enough. So, I confided in him about the secret cellar, where we had discovered the small iron box. Inside was a booklet meant only for the Dingle family descendants. Mr. Villin listened intently, 'That's it! There must be something peculiar about that booklet!'"

"As we spoke, the old servant returned with Isaam from the street. Seeing him, my grief overwhelmed me, and I clung to Isaam, weeping. Mr. Villin was there, but I hardly noticed his actions as I cried. He seemed to pace, deep in thought. Once my tears subsided, he suggested, 'Mrs. Dingle, staying here will only deepen your sorrow. Let me buy this house from you at a generous price. Take some time at your parents' place for now, and then use the money to start fresh with your child in a new place.'"

"At the time, I was so lost. The idea of staying in that house without Asim was unbearable, so I agreed. I assumed the gold was payment for the house, but days later, Mr. Villin provided a substantial sum, claiming it was the true price."

I interjected, puzzled, "Wait a moment, you left your home then?"

"Yes," Mrs. Dingle confirmed. "I took nothing except Isaam, and two old servants accompanied us. One carried the gold as we left."

"This—this seems rather unusual, doesn't it?" I remarked.

Mrs. Dingle paused, as if considering this for the first time. "Yes, it was unusual. But in my grief, I blamed the house for Asim's death. If not for the secret cellar and the book within, he might never have left for Harrogate."

"You had no concrete proof that the book prompted Mr. Dingle's departure?" I asked.

"What else could it have been?" Mrs. Dingle insisted. "His life was ordinary until he discovered the book, and then everything changed."

I nodded, finding her reasoning sound. Mrs. Dingle added, "Asim's death filled me with such revulsion for the house that I couldn't bear to stay. That's why I left so abruptly."

"Understood," I said, accepting her explanation.

Mrs. Dingle continued, "As I reached the door, Mr. Villin approached, asking for my parent's address. I provided it, and he inquired, 'May I live in the house?' I replied, 'It's yours now; do as you wish.' Mr. Villin, being the gentleman he was, expressed his intent to investigate the house, curious about Asim's behavior. I told him, 'Feel free, even tear it down if you like.' And so, I left."

Mrs.Dingle recounted, "After Asim's death, I returned to my parents' home. They were devastated by the news, and our household was in disarray for days. I never returned to that house; instead, I sent a servant to gather some belongings. The servant mentioned that Mr. Villin had been residing in the house."

I inhaled sharply. Uncle Four had indeed been delayed for a month before coming back, meaning he spent at least three weeks in that house. Did he uncover the reason behind Asim Dingle's peculiar actions during his stay?

Curious, I asked, "Did you ever see Mr. Villin again?"

"Yes," Mrs. Dingle replied. "He returned a few days later with a large sum of money and took Isaam shopping. During that visit, he asked me, 'Mrs. Dingle, were Mr. Dingle's ancestors part of the Luddites?' I confirmed, 'Yes, otherwise, they wouldn't have built their homes here.' Mr. Villin then revealed, 'I found and read the booklet!' I was shocked and asked, 'Then why did Asim seek you out for a piece of wood?'"

Mr. Villin explained, 'He wasn't after wood; he sought a specific tree, but it was cut down by our people a month before his arrival, so he settled for wood.' I was bewildered by his explanation. With Asim gone, I had little interest in delving deeper, so I let the matter rest."

"Mr. Villin left, but about two weeks later, he returned to say goodbye, urging me to take care of myself," Mrs. Dingle continued.

"His demeanor was strange, as though burdened by something unsaid. I encouraged him to speak freely. After some hesitation, he advised, 'No matter how many years pass, if you hear of someone selling something—'"

"Mr. Morris, his words were peculiar," Mrs. Dingle said, recalling the moment. "He continued, 'I can't specify what it is now, but it's certainly not something valuable. The price will be high. It might be wood, charcoal, bone, or ash. If you can, you should buy it.'"

Mrs. Dingle said this and looked at me.

I nodded, puzzled by Uncle Four's cryptic message. But from Fernsby's account, I knew Uncle Four had discovered charcoal at the Autumn kiln. At the time, even he was unsure what he would find. Yet, he was convinced there was something significant in the kiln. Why?

I shook my head, mystified.

Mrs. Dingle, too, was perplexed. "Many things Mr. Villin said remain unclear to me," she admitted.

"The entire situation is shrouded in mystery," I agreed. "Please continue."

Mrs. Dingle sighed, "I asked him, 'Why should I buy something if even you don't know what it is?' Mr. Villin sighed, saying, 'I'll find it and send you a letter.'"

"Did you receive his letter?" I asked eagerly.

"Yes, it contained only the word 'charcoal,'" Mrs. Dingle replied.

I pressed further, "Did he ever explain why Mr. Dingle risked his life for that piece of wood?"

"I asked, but Mr. Villin seemed reluctant to answer. He paced and sighed, muttering, 'I don't believe it, I really don't.' I asked, 'What don't you believe?' Mr. Villin said, 'Your husband saw records of a strange event and believed it, but I can't.' When I pressed further, he advised, 'It's better you don't know. Let your child decide when he's older.'"

Mrs. Dingle said, "Before leaving, Mr Villin gave me another item. It was a small, flat box, about the size of a book. Made of iron, its mouth was welded shut. He told me, 'You must take good care of this. No matter where you plan to move, keep it with you. When you get what I just mentioned, you can ask Isaam to open it.' His expression grew even more puzzled as he continued, 'I don't understand – I haven't learned much. Make sure Isaam studies hard; maybe he will understand. He will understand in the future.'"

I was intrigued and asked, "Did you ever inquire what was in the box?"

"I did, but he simply said, 'I don't understand,'" Mrs. Villin replied.

"Is the box still in your possession?" I asked urgently.

Mrs. Dingle nodded, relieving me. The box, at Uncle Four's insistence, must hold something crucial.

I was tempted to ask Mrs. Dingle to fetch the box immediately, but she continued, "After agreeing to Mr. Villin's request, I left with Isaam and the money he provided. We moved first to Singapore, then to Brunei, starting anew. Isaam was diligent. Years later, I saw an ad for charcoal for sale, remembered Mr. Villin's words, and sent for Isaam—"

I interrupted, "I'm aware of what happened when Isaam met Bian Five and Fernsby Three. The deal fell through."

"Yes," Mrs. Dingle confirmed. "Asim returned, saying they demanded an equal volume in gold for the charcoal. He found it absurd."

Throughout Mrs. Dingle's account, I sensed an inexplicable tension. The booklet found in the cellar seemed to trigger Asim Dingle's odd behavior. Uncle Four, Villin, after spending considerable time in the house, might have read it, reacting with disbelief and confusion.

Before leaving, Uncle Four entrusted Mrs. Dingle with an iron box, emphasizing its importance. It likely contained the booklet—an undeniable conclusion.

But why had Mrs. Dingle refrained from opening it all these years?

Observing her clutching the piece of charcoal, it was clear she wasn't merely reminiscing about her husband. The charcoal stirred memories of the past, not because she understood its significance, but because it was a link to a time when everything changed. I resolved to uncover the truth and cut through the lingering mystery. As Mrs. Dingle prepared to speak again, I interrupted, almost impolitely, "Where is the iron box? Please, bring it out."

Startled, Mrs. Dingle recalled, "Mr. Villin said Isaam could open it when interested."

I pressed, "After all these years, haven't you been curious? Haven't you wanted to know?"

Her smile was bitter. "I suspect it holds the book Asim found in the cellar, meant only for Dingle family descendants."

Frustrated, I chuckled, "Mr. Dingle may have died because of this book, yet you adhere to tradition?"

"Precisely because of Asim's death, I wanted Isaam to be the one to read it," Mrs. Dingle explained.

I found myself involuntarily waving my hands, almost uttering, "How can this be?" Old Mrs. Dingle spoke again, her voice tinged with frustration, "Ever since Isaam was old enough to understand, I've talked to him about this. Countless times, yet he remains obstinate, utterly uninterested!"

I sprang to my feet, incredulous. "This involves his father's death. How can he not care?"

Before I could process her words further, Isaam Dingle's voice cut through the air behind me. "Why should I care? The man's dead. Knowing how he died won't change anything. I've left that life behind, built something entirely new. Why let ghosts of the past haunt me now?"

His sudden appearance startled me. I turned to face him, digesting his words. They were not without reason. Although my curiosity was piqued, I could see his point.

Isaam Dingle continued, "When I was ten, my mother urged me to open the iron box and discover its contents. I refused. She asked me every year, and every year I refused. I never wanted to know what lay inside."

I processed his statement quickly. "If you don't want to know, no one will force you. But I must confess, I do want to know."

Isaam Dingle shrugged, "Fine, but that's your concern, not mine."

His nonchalance was unexpected. Despite our brief acquaintance, I could sense his shrewdness. Such people rarely make concessions easily. I scrutinized him, anticipating more.

Sure enough, Isaam Dingle spoke again, "You can have the iron box—"

He gestured towards a piece of charcoal in Mrs. Dingle's grasp, "In exchange for that."

His proposition shocked me to my core. Anger surged, and I nearly struck him. Mrs. Dingle interjected, her voice grating, "Isaam, that's not possible. This charcoal is meant to be traded for an equal volume of gold. At the very least, you'll need to cover their travel expenses too!"

Her audacity pushed me over the edge. I strode towards Mrs. Dingle, my face surely a mask of fury. She stared at me, wide-eyed, as I seized the charcoal and turned to leave.

At the doorway, I paused, addressing Isaam Dingle. "You may disregard the past, but I must tell you—your father perished in the charcoal kiln. Everything turned to ash, save for this piece of charcoal. It holds mysteries, all tied to your father."

I emphasized my final words.

Isaam Dingle's cold reply left me speechless. "Even if you brought my father's corpse, I wouldn't pay your price. Keep it."

Mrs. Dingle pleaded, "Isaam, discuss this with Mr. Morris. It concerns your father—"

Isaam cut her off, "Mother, you merely want someone to hear your tale. You've told it, and he's heard it. What value does this charcoal hold?"

Mrs. Dingle sighed, her silence weighing heavily. I found myself amused by the absurdity of it all.

With nothing left to say, I exited Isaam Dingle's house, my mind a storm of anger, confusion, and unresolved questions.

As I trudged along the road that Isaam Dingle's car had previously navigated, I realized just how far I'd have to walk back to the city. The sheer distance was daunting, but returning to plead with Isaam Dingle was out of the question. My thoughts seethed with frustration at my unexpected predicament. Mrs. Dingle's excitement upon seeing me had been misleading; she knew nothing of the charcoal's secrets, seeking only an audience for her tale.

Despite my usual self-assuredness, I'd found myself mired in this foolish situation. My anger simmered as I continued down the road, and in a fit of irritation, I kicked a stone with all my might. It soared through the air, only to collide with the windshield of an approaching luxury car with a sharp "slap."

The car swerved violently, its tires skidding towards the edge of the road, narrowly avoiding the adjacent field. The driver's skill was evident as the vehicle came to a halt just in time. My heart sank with guilt—my anger had nearly caused a catastrophe.

Rushing towards the car, intent on apologizing sincerely, I was caught off guard when two burly men emerged, fists already swinging. Their aggression was palpable, and their martial prowess unmistakable. A less experienced person would have been overwhelmed in seconds.

Reacting swiftly, I sidestepped a punch, using my foot to trip one of the men, causing him to lurch forward, inadvertently striking his companion. I spun around, bracing for their next assault when a voice rang out behind me, commanding, "Stop! God, Ash, it's you!"

The men froze, their expressions shifting to confusion. I exhaled, turning to see who had intervened. Emerging from the car was none other than Spring Miracle, my creditor and a prominent figure in Asia. His presence was unexpected, especially under such bizarre circumstances, but his recognition of me was evident.

Mr. Miracle's face lit up with a mix of surprise and delight. His unexpected arrival turned the tumultuous encounter into an unexpected reunion.

As Mr. Miracle stepped out of the car and approached me, he grinned and said, "Ash, why are you trying to pick a fight with me? If you really wanted to, my bodyguards would be no match for you!"

His lighthearted comment caught me off guard, dissipating my lingering anger. I couldn't help but laugh. Miracle looked at me, puzzled.

"If I told you I was just venting, and a stray stone I kicked accidentally hit your car, would you believe me?"

Spring was taken aback for a moment, then nodded. "I believe you. You've helped me so much in the past; why wouldn't I trust you? But why are you walking? Where are you headed?"

I sighed, "It's a long story."

Spring clapped me on the shoulder, delighted to have run into me. "It's rare for us to cross paths. How about you join me at the hotel tonight?"

Spring Miracle's influence was undeniable. The car he arrived in was provided by the Sultan himself. As soon as it halted, the bodyguards leaped out, and the driver reported the incident via radio. Within minutes, the rhythmic thump of helicopter blades filled the air—a police helicopter had arrived. The driver exited the car and informed Spring, "Mr. Miracle, the replacement vehicle will be here shortly."

Spring turned to him, "I need two vehicles, one for Mr. Morris, just like the one I'm using."

The driver nodded and returned to make the necessary arrangements. The helicopter circled, then landed, and a group of officers, clearly on high alert, approached. After a brief exchange with the bodyguards, they saluted Spring and glanced at me.

Ignoring their scrutiny, Spring invited me into the car. "What brings you to Brunei, Ash? What strange adventure have you gotten yourself into now?"

I gave a rueful chuckle. "You wouldn't believe it. It's just frustrating. Forget it. Who are you meeting here?"

Spring replied, "A person named Isaam Dingle had asked me for help with a business matter. He begged me to have a meal with him, and I just couldn't turn him down."

I let out a derisive snort. "That guy!"

Spring looked at me, surprised. "Why? Is he not reputable?"

Though tempted to vent my frustrations about Isaam, I held back. "That's between him and me. If you're doing business with him, know that he's competent and will ensure both of you profit. He's sharp, capable, and unwavering. You can count on him."

Spring seemed impressed by my assessment. "I trust your judgment, Ash, but you seemed displeased—"

"It's a long story," I interrupted, then shifted gears. "Curious what I did with the five million dollars you loaned me?"

Spring chuckled, "I don't usually lend money, but for you, I made an exception."

Grateful for his trust, I revealed the charcoal. "I invested in this."

Spring's eyes widened with disbelief as he studied the charcoal. I laughed and said, "I'm afraid you don't have time to hear all the details. It would take at least half a day to explain!"

"You really are something else, Ash."

Just then, a convoy of luxury cars arrived, their occupants greeting Spring warmly. It seemed they were also headed to Isaam Dingle's gathering.

Half an hour later, two opulent RVs pulled up—one for Spring and the other for me. We parted ways, and I drove into the city, checked into a hotel, and stewed in my thoughts. I considered calling Flora but hesitated. What could I possibly say—that I botched a simple task and nearly got thrown out as a fraud? I set the phone down, opting to brood in silence.

Just as I was about to sleep, a knock at the door startled me. I opened it to find Isaam Dingle, looking apprehensive and clutching a paper bag.

I realized Spring must have mentioned me. "Finished with the banquet, Mr. Dingle?"

Asim Dingle hesitated. "May I come in?"

Gesturing for him to enter, he handed me the paper bag. "Mr. Morris, this is the iron box my mother mentioned, given to her by Mr. Villin before he left."

I'd always known Asim Dingle was astute. By offering the iron box immediately, he disarmed my anger, knowing my curiosity would win out. I took it, surprised. "Mr. Dingle, there might be an important family secret inside—"

Asim Dingle cut me off. "I don't want to know. I'm just giving it to you."

His certainty left me speechless, "Well, thank you."

He smiled. "No, I should thank you. Mr. Miracle has appointed me as his agent in Brunei, thanks to your endorsement. Many vied for this role, yet I got it because of you."

"That's due to your own merit," I replied, feeling a sense of closure, even as new mysteries unfolded.

Asim Dingle continued with a warm smile, "Mr. Dingle has numerous ventures here, some with tremendous growth potential. I'd like to invite you to be a consultant."

I was caught off guard. "But I have no experience in business!"

Asim Dingle chuckled, "The consultant's travel expenses are $500,000 annually, and you can receive them in advance for ten years."

The implication dawned on me, and I laughed. "Perfect! This way, I can repay Spring Miracle. Alright, I'll take the position!"

The resolution came as a pleasant surprise. Asim Dingle was visibly pleased and promptly handed me a bank draft. Just as I accepted it, there was another knock at the door. Opening it, I found Spring walking in. Seeing Asim Dingle, he grinned, "You beat me here!"

Asim Dingle stood respectfully, as if in the presence of a superior. I announced, "I've just become Mr. Dingle's consultant."

Spring beamed, "Fantastic! Now I can invest with greater confidence."

Handing Spring the promissory note from Asim Dingle, I said, "Here's your repayment. No interest needed."

Spring accepted it, tucking it into his bag. "I postponed a meeting to catch up with you. What's the story with the charcoal?"

He settled into a chair as he spoke, while Asim Dingle remained standing.

I was elated, having cleared my debt and obtained the intriguing iron box Uncle four gave to Mrs. Dingle. My curiosity piqued, I unceremoniously pulled Spring from his seat and nudged him toward the door. "Apologies, I can't chat right now!"

Spring sighed dramatically, "Everyone's so busy these days!"

He exited, and Asim Dingle quickly followed suit. Once alone, I eagerly shut the door and unwrapped the iron box. Just as Mrs. Dingle described, it was crudely sealed, the welds rough and clearly handmade.

The box appeared to be crafted from a thick iron plate, about a centimeter thick, and I was confident I could pry it open. I retrieved my multi-purpose knife and began filing away at the weld. Iron filings accumulated as I worked, and after about ten minutes, a crack appeared.

Utilizing the knife, I wedged it into the gap, applying force. Gradually, the crack widened. With pliers in hand, I clamped onto one end, bracing myself against the box, and pulled upwards. Slowly, a section of the top began to peel away.

Upon prying open the iron box, I was greeted by a flat package meticulously wrapped in oilcloth. My anticipation heightened as I carefully unwrapped it, revealing a small, unassuming booklet within.

In that moment, I realized why Mrs. Dingle referred to it as a "booklet" rather than a book. It was an old-style account book, crafted from jade button paper adorned with red vertical stripes—an artefact from a bygone era. The cover bore two lines of ominous script: "If the descendants of the Dingle family find this book, it is hard to predict whether it will be a disaster or a blessing——"

The handwriting was indeed as neat as Mrs. Dingle had described. However, contrary to her account, there were additional lines inscribed beside them. In a spirited, albeit uneven hand, Uncle Four had penned:

"I have read everything recorded in this book in detail. While I don't believe or fully understand it, I can confirm that Mr. Asim Dingle was killed due to the strange behavior resulting from reading this book. Even if the ascendants of the Ding family believe it as Mr. Asim Dingle did after reading this book, they should not do foolish things again. Villin Four."

These words clearly reflected Uncle Four's bewilderment and caution after perusing the contents. I had yet to delve into the booklet myself, so the full weight of his warning was not immediately apparent.

I eagerly thumbed through the pages, discovering that the booklet contained about 70 to 80 pages, each filled with small, tightly packed script. Some entries were composed in meticulous detail, while others were hastily scrawled, giving the impression of a diary.

Excitement coursed through me. The mysteries shrouding Asim Dingle—his abrupt departure and peculiar behavior—were on the verge of being unveiled. Holding the booklet felt like grasping the key to a long-buried secret, one that promised to illuminate the past and perhaps alter the future.

CHAPTER 10

The Mysterious Events
Recorded in the Booklet

I took a deep breath and began to delve into the contents of the diary. It was indeed a diary, chronicling events over a span of about three months. The words were numerous—more than 200,000 in total—and by the time I finished reading, the night had turned to midnight. I sat there, my hands resting on the closed booklet, overwhelmed by a sense of profound shock.

Describing the impact of its revelations is challenging, yet it's more beneficial to share the essence of the diary itself. The entries were plentiful, and while copying them verbatim would have been ideal, much was irrelevant to the core story. The writing was disjointed, laden with contemporary references of the time, and the style resembled a semi-literate tone from many years ago, making it quite laborious to comprehend.

Thus, I distilled the main points, omitting extraneous details, and translated some archaic terms into modern equivalents for clarity.

The diary's author was Uber Dingle, whom I surmised was an ancestor of Asim Dingle—perhaps his grandfather or great-grandfather. Uber Dingle served as a senior officer during the Luddite uprisings. His position, as per the diary, was akin to a division's chief of staff in today's military. He was under the command of General Ludd. The diary began in March 1811, during a time when the Luddite movement was at its peak.

In March, government forces had reclaimed Nottingham and Derby. Meanwhile, the northern advance of the Luddites was thwarted by Major-General Byng, yet they maintained control over Manchester. Yorkshire and Lancashire remained within their sphere of influence, bolstered by substantial troop numbers.

The British government had stationed forces near Manchester, led by General FitzRoy, known as the Manchester Brigade, and near Leeds, led by Colonel Thompson, known as the Leeds Brigade. The Manchester

Brigade targeted General Ludd's forces, while the Leeds Brigade opposed Captain King.

Uber Dingle, as an officer under General Ludd, meticulously documented the onset of the bloody conflict with General FitzRoy's Manchester Brigade. His detailed accounts of tactical maneuvers, skirmishes, and full-scale battles provide invaluable insights into this historical period, though they are not central to our story.

The critical turning point was on the eighth day of April. On that day, Uber Dingle recorded a pivotal encounter (I translated it into modern vernacular, yet preserving his first-person perspective):

"General Ludd summoned me to his tent. At that time, our forces were stationed north of Manchester, having notched several victories and captured numerous of FitzRoy's men. Those who surrendered were integrated into our ranks. Among them were 37 officers, chained and detained, slated for execution. General Ludd likely wanted to discuss this matter.

Upon entering the tent, General Ludd dismissed his attendants, his demeanor troubled. He paced for a while before asking, 'What do you foresee for the Luddite movement's future?' I replied, 'Defeat the Leeds Brigade, and we can seize the opportunity to advance north, joining with the besieged forces to forge a new path.'

General Ludd offered a bitter smile, 'I'm worried about the instability in Manchester.' His concern fell into silence. General Ludd's waning popularity in Manchester was whispered about in the ranks, yet I refrained from commenting.

General Ludd pressed on, 'And if our forces are vanquished?' I declared, 'I will lead the death squad to ensure your safety!' He sighed, 'I hope to retire as a wealthy man when the storm passes.' His ambitions left me speechless.

After a lengthy pause, he asked, 'Uber, will you undertake a mission for me?'

'I am at your service!' I pledged.

General Ludd scrutinized me, then abruptly called out, 'Come here!' A captain ushered in sixteen soldiers. I recognized them as General Ludd's elite guards, each a formidable warrior. Pointing at me, General Ludd commanded, 'From this moment, you are to follow Uber's orders without fail!'"

This marked the beginning of a profound and mysterious task, the implications of which were yet to be unveiled.

All seventeen men nodded in agreement. General Ludd dismissed them with a wave of his hand, then unfurled a map across the table, pointing to a spot marked "Ashfield." "This place," he said, "is merely four miles from our camp. We can reach it by crossing two hills."

I scrutinized the map, puzzled. The small valley seemed strategically insignificant—neither defensible nor useful for offensive maneuvers. Why General Ludd drew attention to it baffled me.

His gaze fixed on me, eyes alight with intensity. This was the look he wore when contemplating a monumental decision. My heart quickened; whatever General Ludd intended for me was far from ordinary.

After a long pause, he spoke. "Uber, you are the only one I trust."

I quickly assured him, "No matter the challenge, I will give my utmost."

"Good," he replied, turning to extract an object from a wooden cabinet. It was a cylindrical tube, five inches in diameter and about three feet long, its ends sealed and the body forged from iron.

My curiosity piqued. "What is this? Some new weapon from the foreign powers?" I inquired, mindful of the foreign forces aiding the British government against us.

General Ludd gave a wry smile. "No, this iron cylinder contains treasures I've accumulated over years of warfare."

His words took me aback. General Ludd's campaigns had spanned the affluent regions of the north, and while looting was not uncommon among military leaders, the treasures presented to him by eager subordinates seeking favor likely included rare and invaluable items. The contents of this cylinder, I surmised, were beyond extraordinary.

Seeing my reaction, General Ludd continued, "Uber, this tube holds pearls, jade, diamonds, and other rare gems. By my estimate, it's worth about three million pounds sterling."

I inhaled sharply. "In that case, once the chaos subsides, you'd be more than just a wealthy man!"

His smile was tinged with irony. I ventured, "Do you wish for me to find someone to safeguard these treasures?"

He interrupted with a dismissive gesture, "No need. I've already chosen a secure place to store them."

His assurance left me intrigued, the weight of his plan pressing upon me with newfound urgency. Whatever

General Ludd had in mind for these treasures, it was bound to be as extraordinary as the man himself.

I suddenly realized, "In the valley of Ashfield?"

General Ludd nodded. "Yes. A month ago, while surveying the area, I discovered a secluded spot with towering ancient trees. I devised a plan to conceal the treasures. By hollowing out the core of one of these trees with precision, we can insert the cylinder. The hollow is then filled with a section of another tree's trunk, wrapped with sphagnum moss and soil."

As he explained, I grasped the genius of the method. "In less than a year, the grafted trunk will merge seamlessly with the original, leaving no trace."

General Ludd smiled. "Exactly. The tree will continue to grow, safeguarding the treasure within, hidden from all."

Yet, his assertion that "no one knows" left me uneasy. He knew, I knew, and it required more than one person to execute. Why claim no one knew? I didn't dwell on it at the time.

General Ludd continued, "Uber, I assigned you a team for this task. Speak of it to no one. Once completed, breathe not a word. If defeat befalls us, take the treasure and flee. We'll share it."

His sincerity struck me, stirring both gratitude and nervousness. "I pledge my lifelong service to you, General," I declared.

General Ludd patted my shoulder, handing me a map of Ashfield, and instructed me to begin at dawn. Before departing, I was to retrieve the treasure cylinder from his tent. Despite his warnings to keep silent, my diary habit compelled me to document our conversation, ensuring future generations would know I spoke to no one.

(Reading this diary entry, I was astounded. Asim Dingle's ancestor, a high-ranking officer in the Luddite movement, had undertaken a secret mission for General Ludd, involving a treasure estimated at three million pounds sterling—a staggering fortune, especially given the exponential increase in the value of rare treasures over a century. Asim Dingle's journey to Ashfield likely sought this treasure.)

(This notion seemed plausible, yet as I continued reading, I realized the treasure was but one motive for Asim Dingle's journey to Harrogate; subsequent events unfolded even more bizarrely.

Returning to Uber's diary, the entry following his discussion with General Ludd revealed:)

That sleepless night, I pondered our army's bleak prospects. Even General Ludd anticipated retreat. What path lay before me?

The next morning, I visited General Ludd's tent. Outside, the soldiers and captain awaited. Inside, General Ludd entrusted me with the cylinder, wrapped in a yellow flag. "Remember, Uber, only you and I know of this."

I mentioned the seventeen men outside, but he cut me off quietly, "Their fate is mine to decide. Do not concern yourself."

His words chilled me. I realized General Ludd intended to eliminate witnesses, yet I concealed my shock to avoid suspicion, merely agreeing, "As you see fit."

General Ludd sent me off, the captain already with horses ready. We rode out, the soldiers in two groups of eight. Chatting along the way, I learned the captain, Smith, hailed from Yorkshire. Though respectful, I sensed a sinister depth. Yet at that moment, I couldn't foresee the imminent upheaval.

A few miles from camp, we paused for a break at the base of the hills. As soldiers ate, I drank water, asking the captain, "Do you know the task entrusted to us?"

Unexpectedly, he replied, "No. The general instructed me to follow your lead."

This revelation surprised me, suggesting General Ludd's genuine trust in me as his confidant. A sense of validation washed over me. The captain asked no further questions, and I assured him, "I'll explain upon arrival."

After resting, we advanced into Ashfield. Following the map, we located the tree. The soldiers, equipped with sharp tools, quickly hollowed the tree's core.

By dusk, the task was done. I unwrapped the yellow flag, inserted the cylinder, and sealed the tree with a section from another trunk, covering it with wet mud. The moon shone brightly overhead.

Throughout, the captain and soldiers remained silent. Stepping back, I surveyed the tree, satisfied. "It's done," I announced.

The captain seemed surprised. "Nothing else?"

I warned, "This is a solemn charge from the general. Speak of it to no one."

He nodded, "Yes, I understand the secrecy required."

His twitching eyebrows and anomalous demeanor under the moonlight unsettled me. "The general's trust in you is evident. Take care," I advised.

The captain agreed, "Promoted by the general, I am bound to obey his orders."

I dismissed his words casually, "Of course."

Suddenly, the captain drew his sword, its blade gleaming in the moonlight. Shocked, I stood speechless as he declared, "Mr. Dingle, forgive me, but this is by the general's secret command!"

As the blade descended, instinct propelled me to turn, but pain seared my back. Stumbling, I clung to the tree, my mind reeling. Darkness enveloped my vision, my ears roared, and I realized my life was ending. The general silenced me—tyranny's ruthless hand.

In that moment of despair, consciousness slipped away, yet strangely, my senses returned with clarity. The pain vanished, my body felt weightless, and my mind serene, as if enlightened. The scene before me, vivid yet unfamiliar, unfolded as if from elsewhere. Sounds reached my ears, yet their source eluded me. The first sight was myself, still clutching the tree, blood pouring from my back, my expression pained yet oddly detached. Amusement tinged my thoughts; I felt no pain, so why did I appear so tormented?

Then came anguished cries, and I saw the sixteen soldiers, locked in combat. Eight lay fallen, some twisted, others crawling, bloodied and muddied—a gruesome tableau of Asura hell, their screams chilling the night air.

The battlefield was a cacophony of clashing swords and desperate cries. Amidst the chaos, the soldiers fought with unwavering ferocity, their blades a blur of steel. Yet, one by one, they succumbed to the inevitable, collapsing onto the blood-soaked earth. Only the captain remained, his sword gleaming ominously in the dying light.

I watched as the captain moved with grim determination, inspecting each fallen comrade. Those who still clung to life were swiftly dispatched, his sword delivering the final silence to all sixteen. Then, with a deliberate stride, he approached where my lifeless body was propped against a tree. He raised his sword as if to strike, but hesitation gripped him. His breath escaped in a heavy sigh, the sword lowering as he whispered, "If this is the order, do not hold it against me, Lord Dingle."

His words lingered in the air, a chilling testament to his fate. I could see him wipe the blood from his blade onto his shoe, oblivious to the doom that awaited him at General Ludd's camp. I yearned to warn him, but my voice was lost. Was I even capable of speech, or had my very essence dissolved? My body remained there, bound to the tree, yet my awareness floated free, untethered. In that moment of clarity, it hit me—I was dead. My soul had abandoned its earthly vessel.

I was dead!

(As I delved into Uber Dingle's diary, a shiver coursed through me. The dim hotel room seemed to dim further, shadows creeping into corners. It was astonishing, this revelation. How could Uber Dingle, declared dead, have penned his own demise? The handwriting was unmistakably his, consistent throughout. Could the dead truly write?

His account of death was mystifying, painting a picture of a consciousness adrift—devoid of eyes, ears, or mouth, yet perceiving all. My palms grew clammy, leaving a damp imprint on the pages as I lifted them. I forced myself to breathe, to steady my racing heart, knowing the narrative would only spiral further into the unknown.

Uber Dingle's diary promised revelations yet to come, each entry a key to unlocking the enigma that lay ahead. I braced myself for the journey, aware that the most profound mysteries were still to be unveiled.)

In the shadow of the ancient tree, I found myself untethered from my mortal coil. My soul had drifted free, yet silence enveloped me. I yearned to scream, to chase after the captain as he disappeared into the mist, but found myself rooted, unable to venture beyond the tree's wide-reaching branches.

I rose and sank within this arboreal prison, exploring its heights and depths. From the tree's crown, I observed the captain's tortured retreat, his backward glances tinged with guilt and despair, until he vanished from the valley's embrace.

Descending again, I witnessed the twisted visage of my own lifeless form, still gripping the tree with a deathly embrace. Realization dawned: my soul had taken refuge within the tree, confined to its wooden heart. The thought was suffocating. Desperation clawed at me as I struggled to break free, but my cries were swallowed by the void.

Time lost meaning in my struggle, a nightmare of fragmented memories. Suddenly, darkness overwhelmed me, pain seared through my body, and I screamed—a sound! My senses flooded back as I reentered my corporeal form, clinging to the tree with hands bloodied and trembling.

The agony was relentless, but training took over. I tore fabric from my garments, binding my wounds with practiced hands. Exhaustion claimed me as I collapsed, yearning for the release of death once more. Yet, life clung stubbornly, the world blurring in and out of consciousness.

When the stars reappeared, illuminating the night, I pondered my impossible revival. Perhaps the captain's strike had lacked fatal precision, sparing my vital organs. Or perhaps my soul's desperate struggle had inadvertently reignited my body's dormant spark.

My days became a cycle of pain and fainting, until a woodcutter stumbled upon the grim tableau. His timely aid pulled me back from the brink, and I found solace and recovery in the quiet of his care.

As strength returned, I bid farewell to my saviors, venturing back to the deserted camp. The tent remained as I'd left it, a ghost of my former life. Alone, I resolved to abandon the military, to turn my back on the general who had betrayed me, and claim the treasure hidden within the tree.

At Ashfield Valley, the skeletal remains of soldiers greeted me, guardians of the silent tree.

The tree loomed before me, its ancient bark concealing secrets buried deep within. With careful hands, I peeled away the mud, preparing to pry open its hidden heart. Yet, as the knife slid into the gap, a strange force propelled me forward, colliding with the trunk. In an instant, I was outside myself, observing my body, its face twisted in avarice and glistening with sweat, as it crumpled to the ground.

A surreal clarity washed over me. My soul had departed, yet no violence had severed it. This was the release I had craved in my darkest hours of suffering, a liberation denied until now. Caught between worlds, I grappled with the choice—remain entwined with the tree or reclaim my flesh.

In that fleeting moment, understanding enveloped me like a warm embrace. Though I could not hear my laughter, joy coursed through my being. Like sages of old who found truth in a flash of insight, I had glimpsed a profound reality.

The soul within the tree and the soul within the body were one, indistinguishable in their essence. Whether rooted in wood or flesh, the spirit remained constant. Why cling to rigid distinctions? As long as the soul endures, the tree is the body, and the body is the tree.

A gentle breeze swept through the valley, and my fallen form rose again, eyes perceiving not my own limbs but the steadfast tree. I spoke, and my voice resonated through the air—my soul had returned to its earthly vessel, unified once more.

This newfound enlightenment rendered material wealth meaningless, ephemeral as clouds drifting across the sky.

The bones of the fallen, the leaves scattered on the ground, all were part of my being. The corporeal form may last a century, the ancient tree a millennium, but what truly persists?

Eternity resides in the unseen, in the boundless realm of the spirit. To grasp this truth is to touch the edge of immortality.

I drifted away, and for me, there was nothing to be attached to.

* * *

The most poignant entry in Uber Dingle's diary encapsulates his extraordinary journey and the revelations that followed. As I immersed myself in his words, I grappled with an indescribable mix of awe and disbelief. His narrative of traversing the boundaries between life and death illuminates a fundamental truth: the body is transient, and life, by its nature, is ephemeral.

But what truly captivated me was his account of the soul, this ethereal essence that twice found sanctuary within the confines of a tree. What unfathomable force orchestrated such a phenomenon?

In a world where the soul is often spoken of as intangible, Uber Dingle's experience defied the ordinary, as his soul moved freely within the tree's expansive reach, yet remained tethered to its form. This raises an intriguing question: if the tree became his body, would he feel pain if its bark was breached or branches severed?

Uber Dingle left this question unanswered, perhaps because no one was present to challenge his arboreal sanctuary. Yet, his singular experience begs another question: what of the sixteen soldiers who perished alongside him? Where did their souls find refuge?

The notion of souls inhabiting trees or other objects resonates with ancient lore, where spirits cling to nature's fabric. Yet, Uber Dingle's precise account stands alone in its vivid detail.

Reflecting on these mysteries, I understand why Uncle Four was left with only disbelief and confusion. Were I to be asked my opinion, I too would echo his sentiment, "I don't believe it" and "I don't understand."

As I sat pondering, I resumed reading the diary. Uber Dingle's later years were described with stark simplicity, as if he had truly embraced the fleeting nature of existence. Even his marriage was noted with detached brevity: "Couldn't avoid living an ordinary human life and marrying a wife."

Towards the end, an addendum appeared, written on paper of a slightly different texture, suggesting it was added at a later date. What new insights or revelations might it contain?

These pages capture the final days of Uber Dingle's life. Allow me to recount his reflections:

"I am old now, my physical strength waning, and my body nearing its end. Over the past six months, I've tirelessly sought to free my soul from its corporeal confines, yet success eludes me. Once, I isolated myself for four days and nights, teetering on the brink of death from starvation. My abdomen felt as though pierced by knives, my body feeble and frail, but still, my soul remained bound.

Suicide crossed my mind, a seemingly simple escape from this mortal shell. But the uncertainty loomed—would my soul find freedom, or remain trapped? After much contemplation, I concluded that my only hope lies in returning to the old place.

Twice, my soul found refuge within a great tree, lingering in its ancient embrace. In hindsight, it was less than ideal, yet the tree's thousand-year longevity surpasses my failing body. Perhaps there, I might unravel the secret of traversing freely, of attaining immortality.

I leave this world with no regrets, the future an enigma. I dare not predict what awaits, I dare not."

The final paragraph is succinct, an indication of Uber Dingle's acceptance of his fate. After penning these words, it seems he departed for Ashfield Valley.

Beneath Uber Dingle's account lies another sheet, penned by his descendant Asim Dingle, offering his reflections upon reading the diary. I'll recount his thoughts:

"This kind of thing is really unbelievable, so it can only be regarded as an extra chapter of 'Grimm's Fairy Tales.'"

(To Asim Dingle, the tale seemed fantastical. His initial reaction one of disbelief, a natural response.)

"Yet, upon a second reading, doubt crept in. The meticulous detail and care with which Uber Dingle documented his experiences suggested purpose, not whimsy. The booklet, hidden with such deliberation, was not merely a product of idle fancy."

Asim Dingle pondered the implications: "If the descendants of the Dingle family find this book, it is hard to predict whether it will be a disaster or a blessing——" The question lingered. Would those who uncovered its secrets, like Uber Dingle, seek liberation in the ancient tree's embrace, risking body and soul for a chance at transcendence?

Asim Dingle's contemplation of his ancestor's mystical experiences led him down a path of deep introspection and curiosity. His initial skepticism slowly transformed into a profound inquiry about the nature of the soul and its potential to transcend the physical body.

"Did Uber Dingle succeed?" Asim Dingle wondered. "A century is but a blink for a venerable tree. If his soul lingers there, what mysteries might it whisper to those who seek its shade? It's truly astonishing to consider." Asim's thoughts began to transcend disbelief, entertaining the possibility that souls could indeed exist independently of the body.

Restless nights followed, filled with a whirl of questions.

If a soul could inhabit a tree, experiencing life anew, did it require a living vessel to maintain such a state?

Could this phenomenon extend beyond plants? Asim's imagination spun wildly: what if a soul became enmeshed in the essence of a fragile blade of grass, or even an animal? Would a soul within a dog experience the world through new senses, or might a soul in a grasshopper flit from leaf to leaf?

The musings grew even more abstract. If souls could also inhabit inanimate objects, what would become of a soul adrift in a mote of dust, swirling through the air? The notion of omnipresence tantalized and bewildered him, stretching the limits of human understanding.

He realized that these thoughts, though fascinating, ventured into realms uncharted by conventional wisdom.

Asim Dingle found himself increasingly absorbed by these musings, his mind occupied by the enigma of existence and the potential for a soul's liberation from the corporeal. In the days following his discovery of the diary, he was consumed by this quest for understanding, unable to share his burgeoning obsession with his wife.

Driven by a newfound resolve, Asim decided to journey to Ashfield Valley, to stand before the ancient tree that had cradled his ancestor's spirit. "If Uber Dingle's soul resides within, will he sense my presence? Could I converse with him? What might a soul appear as? Would I be able to perceive or feel him?"

Fueled by a desire to unravel the mystery, Asim Dingle felt the stirrings of a deep longing within himself. "If the soul can truly transcend the body," he wrote, "I wish to experience it as well." With this determination, his path was set, and his journey into the unknown began.

"To put it another way, even if I cannot solve the mystery of the soul on this trip, at least I can get the treasures of General Ludd, which are priceless. Haha!"

Asim Dingle's resolve to venture to Ashfield Valley was not just driven by the enigmatic promise of spiritual liberation but also by the allure of the Ludd's treasures. Though he jested with a "haha," his deeper understanding of the soul's immortality overshadowed the quest for material wealth. His contemplation led to a profound realization: the ephemeral nature of physical life pales in comparison to the eternal journey of the soul.

He was captivated by the possibility of achieving what he perceived as "immortality" by transcending the physical form.

"I must go to Ashfield to see the big tree. The treasures of General Ludd are truly insignificant in comparison. If the soul can live independent of the body, wouldn't that be 'immortality'?

This is a great temptation. Uber once said, 'It is hard to predict whether it will be a disaster or a blessing.' I believe it will only bring blessings, not disasters. No matter what, I must ensure my soul, like Uber's, leaves my body. Even if my body is damaged, I will not hesitate.

I firmly believe that as long as I hold this conviction and follow Uber's example, I will achieve my goal.

Whether it's a tree, a stone, a blade of grass, or anything else, I will attach my soul to it. I believe this is the first step. The human soul must leave its original body before it can make the second step. What is the second step? I hope to come and go freely and live forever.

I don't fear death. Death is just a way of liberation!

I have decided to go ahead with this. I don't know what the consequences will be, but even if I die, something of me will remain. What remains will be the second form of my life.

I want to leave a few words for Isaam. When he grows up, he should know these things. As for whether he wants to follow in my footsteps and those of Uber, that is up to him to decide.

I am leaving."

This is the last paragraph of Asim Dingle's record.

In this paragraph, his certainty was truly surprising. Although I had read Uber Dingle's record and thought similarly, I did not have such a firm belief. Perhaps it was because Uber Dingle was Asim Dingle's ancestor, and some mysterious and inexplicable genetic factors were involved.

After Asim Dongle's record, there were a few words written by Uncle Four:

"Mr. Asim Dingle is dead. He died in the charcoal kiln of the Charcoal Gang. What is left in the kiln? Is it true that the second stage of his life began there, as Mr. Dingle said? It is really incomprehensible."

"In any case, I decided to take the ominous risk and enter the charcoal kiln to see what was going on. If I find anything, I will inform his wife and son. But the matter is bizarre. No matter what is found, the offspring of the Dingle family has the right to know everything. But it is hard to predict whether it will be a blessing or a curse for anyone to know this. The offspring of the Dingle family should not know it easily, unless they are extremely eager to uncover all the secrets. Otherwise, it is better to keep it unknown to them. As for how to reveal the story to the offspring of the Dingle family when they are extremely eager, I will think about it later."

Uncle Four said at the time, "I will think about it later." Eventually, he came up with a way.

He entered the Autumn charcoal kiln and found that besides ash, there was only a piece of charcoal. Judging from the records of Uber Dingle and Asim Dingle, this piece of charcoal is naturally the "second form" of Asim Dingle's life that he firmly believed in!

When I thought of this, I couldn't help but shudder!

If this is the case, then Asim Dingle's soul is in that piece of charcoal!

As I stood before the box containing the charcoal, apprehension gripped me. Was Asim Dingle truly present within this seemingly mundane object, experiencing existence in a form beyond human comprehension? Could this piece of charcoal, preserved indefinitely, harbor his soul, perceiving and thinking as it lay dormant?

The thought was staggering. If true, it challenged everything I understood about life and the afterlife. There, within reach, was the embodiment of Asim Dingle's quest—a testament to his belief in the soul's enduring journey. Yet, the courage to confront this mystery, to open the box and face the unknown, eluded me. What lay within was a profound enigma, one that blurred the boundaries between life, death, and eternity.

As I pondered the implications of Asim Dingle's soul possibly residing within the charcoal, questions flooded my mind. Would scraping the charcoal cause him pain? Could he see me as I held it? This notion of a "second stage" life, where a soul depends on an object, seemed both a haunting torment and a potential solace.

My confusion was profound, and I found myself admiring the cleverness of Uncle Four's plan. He had devised a way to make Isamm Dingle believe in the incredible narrative by offering to exchange the charcoal for an equal volume of gold. It was a test of conviction—only someone truly convinced would make such an exchange. As for Isaam's lack of interest and disdain for even that booklet, Uncle Four naturally did not anticipate it.

Isaam's dismissive remark, "Even if you bring my father's body, I will not be interested," echoed in my mind. What if I told him it was his father's soul? Would his response change?

With a bitter smile, I knew I wouldn't reveal this to him. As Uncle Four suggested, if Dingle's offspring didn't wish to learn the entire truth, he needn't know at all. The offer of gold in exchange was simply a means to discern true desire.

As I steadied myself, I opened the wooden box and gazed at the unassuming piece of charcoal. Externally, it appeared ordinary, much like the tree that had once cradled Uber Dingle's soul. Its lack of visible anomaly didn't rule out the presence of Asim Dingle's soul within.

Feeling as though I'd taken a plunge into the surreal, I found myself speaking to the charcoal. "Mr. Dingle, if you're truly within this charcoal, according to your ancestors' accounts, you should see and hear me," I said, my voice trembling with uncertainty.

The charcoal remained silent, unmoving. Sweat trickled down my face as I continued, "How can I confirm your existence? If this is the 'second stage' of life, as you claimed, it cannot be the ultimate stage. What is the point of spending eternity in charcoal, devoid of sensation?"

Though I addressed the charcoal, I was really conversing with myself, vocalizing my inner doubts. There were no answers, only the quiet presence of the charcoal.

I spoke at length, as if in a trance, but the charcoal offered no response.

Asim Dingle's journey to Ashfield Valley had led to the discovery that the tree he sought had been felled for charcoal. Bian and Fernsby recounted the events that followed Asim Dingle's arrival at Ashfield, shedding light on his unwavering determination. His leap into the charcoal kiln was an act that seemed beyond the resolve born from mere contemplation. Something profound must have occurred, solidifying his belief in the soul's journey beyond the corporeal.

I was left with a burning question: What transformative experiences did Lin Asim encounter upon reaching his destination? What gave him the courage to embrace such a drastic step, seemingly indifferent to the fate of his physical form?

In my quest for answers, I found myself turning to the charcoal once more, speaking to it repeatedly in the hope of eliciting a response. My solitary vigil stretched through the night, filled with desperate inquiries that only Asim Dingle might answer.

As dawn broke, reality crept back in. I sighed, closed the wooden box, and prepared to leave. The weight of unanswered questions lingered as I quietly departed Brunei, choosing not to inform Spring or Isaam of my departure.

At the airport, Flora's concerned expression greeted me. Her words, "What's wrong with you? You look so pale!" cut through my fog of introspection. I knew my visage must reflect the turmoil within me—a turmoil that had left me questioning the very nature of life and the soul's enduring journey.

CHAPTER 11

There Is a Soul in Charcoal

The experiences I had encountered were so enigmatic and profound that they defied explanation, leaving me at a loss for understanding.

As Flora and I made our way to the garage, I felt an urgency for her to grasp the gravity of what I had discovered.

"I'll drive, and you need to read something immediately!" I insisted, hoping she would immerse herself in the revelations of the booklet during our journey home. However, Flora, ever the voice of reason, declined. "No, I don't think you're in the right state to drive. I'm not as anxious as you. Whatever it is, it can wait until we're home."

Her calm refusal prompted a bizarre thought. What if, in the event of a crash, our souls found themselves inhabiting the wreckage of the car? Would we experience the decay of the metal as a physical affliction, akin to living with a perpetual itch? The absurdity of the notion made me chuckle, drawing a concerned glance from Flora. I quickly reassured her, "Don't worry, I'm fine!"

Once home, anticipation overtook me as I handed Flora the booklet. "Read it, see everything that's recorded here," I urged. With my guidance, she quickly navigated through the crucial details, bypassing the less relevant parts that had initially consumed my time.

When she finished, Flora looked at me with a puzzled expression. "What conclusion did you reach?" she inquired.

I took a moment to compose myself. "What's wrong with you? You should have reached the same conclusion!" I exclaimed, frustrated by her lack of immediate insight.

Despite my insistence, Flora gestured her uncertainty, prompting me to reveal my deduction. "The conclusion is: Asim Dingle's soul is in that piece of charcoal!"

Flora's response, though light-hearted, struck a chord. "That's good," she said with a hint of teasing. "Do you remember Peter? He said there was a person in the charcoal, and you said there was a ghost in the charcoal—"

I was taken aback, my voice almost cracking as I urged Flora to repeat her words. My reaction must have startled her, as she quickly apologized, thinking she'd crossed a line with her joke. But it wasn't her teasing that rattled me; it was the sudden clarity her words had sparked.

"No, it's not that. Please, just say it again," I insisted, eager to grasp the fleeting revelation that had eluded me.

Flora, still a bit puzzled, obliged. "I said that both you and Peter have your points. He mentioned seeing a person in the charcoal, and you said there was a ghost in the charcoal."

Her words set my mind racing. I paced back and forth, piecing together the scattered thoughts. "That's right," I muttered to myself. "Peter claimed to see a person in the charcoal through X-ray exposure. It appeared on the screen and shocked him. And I said there was a ghost?" I paused, the realization dawning on me. "What Peter witnessed and what I inferred—they're the same!"

Flora, observing my epiphany, remained silent, processing this connection. When I pressed her for agreement, she chuckled, "No need to yell; I'm just taken aback."

"You've always been open to new ideas, haven't you?" I questioned, finding comfort in her usual receptiveness.

"Sure," Flora replied with a hint of irony. "A ghost in charcoal, visible on an X-ray screen—it's a concept that's a bit too novel, even for me."

I gestured for her to sit, eager to walk her through my thought process. "Let's break it down. First, do you believe that people have souls, or ghosts exit, if you will?"

Flora met my gaze, contemplating her response. "Do you want a straightforward 'yes' or 'no,' or can I share my thoughts?"

"Of course, share your thoughts," I encouraged, appreciating her perspective.

"Alright," Flora began thoughtfully. "Life ceases and death follows; there's a clear distinction between the living and the dead. The soul, or essence, resides in the living body. So yes, I do believe in the existence of the soul."

Pleased with her openness, I pressed further. "What about Uber Dingle's account? His soul entering a tree?"

Flora pondered this for a moment. "Based on his detailed records, it seems unlikely he fabricated the story. It could be a rare phenomenon, the soul migrating from the body to another form. Even ancient texts have similar tales."

I clapped my hands, invigorated by her acknowledgment. "Exactly! But none are as specific and detailed as Uber Dingle's account."

Flora nodded, a sign of her growing acceptance. Together, we stood on the cusp of understanding, grappling with concepts that stretched the boundaries of known reality—souls, immortality, and the profound mysteries of existence.

As I delved deeper into the implications of Uber Dingle's records and Asim Dingle's subsequent actions, a singular conclusion emerged: the soul, upon death, might find refuge in an object it comes into contact with. Flora, grasping the essence of my thoughts, interjected, "Wait a minute!"

Though I urged her to let me finish, she pressed on, "I know what you're getting at. You're suggesting that when someone dies, their soul might transfer into an object they touch."

"Exactly," I affirmed. "Uber Dingle was stabbed, fell forward, and his soul entered the tree he grasped." Flora pondered this, questioning what Asim Dingle might have done in the charcoal kiln to trigger a similar transfer. She speculated about him embracing wood or leaning against the kiln wall, but I interrupted, "We don't need to assume. All that's left in the kiln is this piece of charcoal. Asim Dingle's soul is in there."

Flora was momentarily silent, then raised a crucial point: "Even if we accept that his soul is in the charcoal, how can we free it?"

I had contemplated this question and replied, "We need help."

"Who?" Flora asked.

"I'll go to London," I declared. "Sir Psori is a member of the Spiritual Society. He's a renowned

scientist with extensive experience in spiritual research. He can help."

Flora agreed that Sir Psori was the right person. As I carefully placed the charcoal back into its box and made my way to the study, Flora accompanied me briefly before leaving me to make the crucial call. Her departure left me alone to focus on reaching out to Sir Psori, despite the late hour in London.

When Sir Psori finally answered, his voice was laced with irritation, which was understandable given the time. I couldn't help but chuckle internally at the situation. I had inadvertently woken him at three in the morning, and even the most composed gentleman might be a bit gruff under such circumstances.

"Who is it? Ash Morris? What the hell?" came Sir Psori's voice.

"Yes, it's me, Ash Morris—the one and only," I declared, hoping to cut through his annoyance. "I do have a ghost from hell in my hand and need your help."

Despite the oddity of my statement, Sir Psori's interest was piqued immediately. The mention of a "ghost" had a way of capturing his attention, and his tone shifted to one of recognition and curiosity.

"Ah, Ash! That Ashi Morris," he exclaimed, his mood lightening. "Sorry, I don't specialize in alien souls." His words showed that he remembered me.

We had crossed paths before, locked in spirited debate amidst the clinking of glasses and murmurs of an intrigued audience. Our topic of choice? The enigmatic creatures from beyond our world.

In an unexpected flourish, he strode confidently to the center of the room, his voice cutting through the ambient chatter like a surgeon's scalpel. "Gentlemen," he proclaimed, "we humans are still in the dark about the mysteries of our own existence. Perhaps our energies are better spent unearthing the enigma within, rather than chasing phantoms across the cosmos."

His words sparked a fire within me, igniting a debate that raged on for what felt like hours. It seemed that our spirited discussion had left a lasting impression on him.

Without missing a beat, Sir Psori inquired, "You mentioned you have a ghost in your hand. What does that mean?"

"It's a long story," I replied, acknowledging the complexity of the situation. "I'm heading to London as soon as possible. Can you gather those with experience in soul research? We need to start as soon as I arrive. I trust you won't refuse."

His laughter was reassuring. "I never refuse a visit from a soul," he assured me.

After confirming my plans to contact him upon arrival, I hung up the phone, feeling a surge of excitement. Sir Psori and his colleagues had invested over two decades in the study of souls, and I was optimistic that their expertise would help unravel the mysteries surrounding Asim Dingle's soul encased in the charcoal. With their assistance, I hoped to uncover not only answers but potentially a way to release and understand the soul's journey.

I packed my bag with swift efficiency, ignoring Flora's gentle insistence that I rest before embarking on my journey. My resolve was unyielding; the plane beckoned, and by day's end, I was airborne, bound for London.

Upon arrival, the scrutiny of the customs officer was palpable, his gaze fixed with suspicion on the innocuous piece of charcoal nestled in my belongings. Soon enough, I found myself escorted to a secluded room, its shelves brimming with enigmatic instruments whose purposes eluded even my imagination.

A police officer greeted me with formal politeness, but I interrupted his preamble with a question of my own: "Is Old Tom still with Scotland Yard?"

His eyes widened with surprise. "You know Old Tom?"

"Indeed," I replied with a knowing nod.

Puzzlement creased his brow. "Old Tom is a senior consultant now. Please, wait a moment."

He stepped out, leaving behind two vigilant officers. Minutes ticked by, and when he returned, his expression was laced with intrigue. I surmised he had just spoken with Old Tom. Confirming my suspicion, he relayed, "Sir, Old Tom said that even if you were carrying an atomic bomb and threatened Buckingham Palace, he'd let you pass."

I chuckled warmly. "Old Tom is an old friend."

The officer shifted uneasily, rubbing his hands together. "But—uh—the charcoal you brought, it's been emitting a very high-frequency sound wave—"

His words propelled me from my seat. Alarm flickered in his eyes. "Did I say something wrong?"

"Show me the test record!" I urged, my voice a blend of urgency and anticipation.

He hesitated, then beckoned a female officer, who handed me a scroll of charts. The waveforms danced across the paper, instantly recognizable, echoing the mysterious patterns from the photographs Peter had entrusted to me.

A myriad of questions swirled in my mind. What did this convergence of waveforms signify? I stood there, a puzzle unsolved, my thoughts a whirlwind.

The officer's voice pierced my contemplation. "Sir, what exactly is inside this piece of charcoal?"

I gave a wry smile, leaning slightly against the counter as I spoke. "I'm telling you, there's a ghost in there. And believe me, this specter doesn't have the proper paperwork for entry."

The officer chuckled, though it was an uneasy sound, betraying his dedication to duty. "Sir," he began with a polite firmness, "despite what you or anyone else claims, we're obligated to conduct a thorough inspection."

Suppressing a yawn, I replied, "That's your prerogative. But handle it with care."If anything happens to it, you, and indeed the whole of the United Kingdom, might find yourselves in an uncomfortable position. You just can't even afford to pay for it."

The officer, displaying that quintessential British humor, nodded in agreement. "Quite right. Britain is indeed too poor," he jested, summoning his assistants to scrutinize the charcoal with an array of sophisticated instruments.

An hour ticked by before he returned, scratching his head, the object still intact in his hands. "Any conclusions?" I inquired.

A rueful smile crept across his face. "None whatsoever."

"Could you at least provide the paper with the high-frequency sound wave data? It might prove useful," I suggested.

He obliged without hesitation, and with that, I exited the airport, hailing a taxi that whisked me straight to Sir Psoli's abode.

Sir Psoli resided in an antiquated apartment, rich with history and lore. Drawn to its reputation as a "haunted house," he'd acquired it for a song when the previous owner fled, unnerved by its spectral occupants. To Psoli, the prospect was thrilling rather than terrifying, a potential treasure trove of ghostly encounters. Yet, reality had proven less obliging.

Despite over a decade of residence, Sir Psoli had yet to witness a single supernatural event. Undeterred, he had even founded a séance society, hoping to commune with the otherworldly. Yet, success remained elusive.

Upon my arrival, it was clear Psoli had made meticulous preparations. He had gathered seven esteemed members of his spiritual society, along with three French mediums renowned for their craft.

As I stepped inside, Sir Psoli rushed forward, grasping my hand with an intensity that bordered on fervor. His face, flushed with anticipation, displayed a youthful eagerness. "Relax," I quipped, "I'm not a soul you know."

Psoli chuckled, his eyes twinkling with a fervent belief. "We all have souls within us," he replied earnestly.

"Well then, considering the number of souls accumulated since time immemorial," I mused, "shouldn't the earth be brimming with them by now?"

Psoli, undeterred by my jest, responded with solemn conviction. "You misunderstand. Souls transcend earthly confines. They can exist anywhere," he declared, pointing skyward to emphasize the vastness beyond our planet.

Realizing the depth of his belief, I dropped the playful banter. Psoli sighed, his gaze drifting wistfully. "Perhaps they dwell too far for easy reach."

"You'll join them eventually," I consoled, a faint smile on my lips.

Psoli seemed momentarily taken aback, then nodded. "Come," he said, gesturing for me to follow. "Let me introduce you to some of my friends."

And so, the evening unfolded, a tapestry of intrigue and anticipation, within the shadowed walls of that enigmatic abode.

As I stood in the dimly lit drawing room, Sir Psoli's friends emerged from the shadows, forming a semicircle behind him. He introduced each one in turn, their names flickering like distant stars in my memory. I shook hands with them, trying to imprint their faces more than their names. Among them was a man named Gint, short and half-bald, with the unmistakable features of a Jew. Little did I know then that Gint's story would unfurl into something peculiar, though unrelated to this "charcoal" saga. That tale, however, is for another time.

Sir Psoli, with a flourish, introduced me to his companions: "This is my friend Ash Morris, who shuttles between Hong Kong and the UK. Actually, he is a man of the world. He has encountered countless enigmas. Like us, he firmly believes in the existence of souls."

Nods of acknowledgement circled the room. One figure stood out—a gaunt man with a pallid complexion, his face naturally cast in shadows that could rival any vampire's. His name was Gan Mins.

As we moved towards the séance room, Gan Mins addressed me with a voice that echoed through the air. "Mr. Morris, may we learn your foundational views on the soul?"

His question caught me off guard—a test of my credibility, no doubt. I could feel the weight of their gazes, each pair of eyes fixed on me, eager to gauge my worthiness.

We entered Sir Psoli's séance room, a cavernous hall dominated by an oval table. The emptiness of the room swallowed us, the dim lights cloaking us in a veil of mystery.

Once seated, all eyes remained on me, awaiting my response. I contemplated for a moment, choosing my words carefully. "To me, the soul is the essence of life," I began.

"Physically, our bodies remain unchanged from life to death, yet something vital departs. That something is the soul."

Gan Mins leaned forward, curiosity piqued. "And what form does this soul take?"

I paused, crafting my analogy with care. "Consider the human body as a mere vessel, a tool facilitating movement and expression. The soul, however, is the true essence, guiding and animating the body. Allow me to illustrate."

I paused again, searching for the perfect metaphor. "Imagine a robot, controlled by a sophisticated computer. It moves, listens, and reacts. The computer's memory is the driving force—change the programming, and the robot's abilities change. Insert a chess program, and it becomes a chess master; a bridge program, and it excels at bridge."

I noticed their rapt attention and continued, "In this analogy, the computer's memory is akin to the soul."

Sir Psoli nodded, his approval evident. "An apt metaphor indeed."

I pressed on, "Remove the computer's memory, and the robot ceases to function, becoming lifeless. This doesn't negate the existence of the memory; it's simply detached from its vessel. The soul is similar—it persists beyond the body. Our task is to discover a means to connect with this memory through unknown channels."

A warm applause followed my explanation, the sound echoing off the walls like a benediction.

As the applause dwindled, I added, "In truth, we know precious little about souls. Their nature remains a mystery. Yet, I am certain of one thing: souls possess an awareness—they perceive and understand, though perhaps not in the ways we do."

Gan Mins interjected, "No!"

I quickly amended, "Perhaps not through sight or hearing as we know it, but if a soul resides here, it is aware of our actions and words."

This time, Gan Mins offered no rebuttal, the silence a testament to a shared understanding of the mysterious realm we sought to explore.

The séance room was charged with anticipation as I shared my unusual theory. "There exists a unique case," I began, "where a soul, upon departing from a human body, may take refuge in a tree, bound to it as its new realm."

Faces around me reflected a spectrum of disbelief, their research having never touched on such an idea. I pressed on,

"And not just trees—other objects can serve as temporary sanctuaries for souls."

As I spoke, I unzipped my travel bag, revealing a wooden box. I carefully opened it and held out the object within—an unassuming piece of charcoal.

"Charcoal!" several voices exclaimed in unison, eyes wide with skepticism.

"Yes," I confirmed, meeting their incredulity with steadfast conviction. "I believe a soul resides within this very piece of charcoal."

The room fell silent, the air thick with curiosity and doubt. Sir Psoli broke the silence first. "What leads you to this belief, my friend?"

I nodded, acknowledging the complexity of my claim. "It's a long and intricate tale. I'll do my best to elucidate."

I paused, gathering my thoughts before diving into the story—a narrative spanning over a century, entangled with the Charcoal Gang and the upheavals of the Luddite movement. It was a tale not easily grasped by contemporary minds, yet I wove it with care, ensuring its essence was conveyed.

Three hours elapsed before my story concluded, leaving the room in a contemplative hush. Gan Mins was the first to speak, though his words were directed at Psoli. "Everything Mr. Morris has shared—"

Psoli interrupted, his voice firm with assurance. "I believe every word that Ash has spoken."

Gan Mins nodded, acknowledging Psoli's trust. "Then we've resolved the primary issue. Based on Mr. Morris's account, it's plausible that Mr. Asim Dingle's soul inhabits this charcoal, though it may also reside elsewhere."

I concurred, "Indeed. But I must remind you, during an X-ray examination, a human-like figure was reportedly seen within the charcoal."

Gan Mins reacted sharply, "No! Souls cannot be seen!"

His fervor ignited my temper. "How can you be so certain?" I challenged. "Your only evidence is your lack of personal experience."

Gan Mins flushed with indignation, poised to retort, but Psoli intervened. "Let's not quarrel. For now, let's assume the soul is within the charcoal. I propose we take a short break, then endeavor to contact Mr. Asim's soul together."

No objections were raised. The charcoal was left on the table as we exited the séance room.

In the room prepared for me, Psoli joined me briefly. "Don't be upset with Gan Mins," he advised. "He's earnest and sometimes stubborn, yet he's a leading authority on soul-world interactions."

I shrugged, the tension easing. "It's fine. I'm not entirely convinced Asim Dingle's soul is in the charcoal. It might just as well be in a brick from the charcoal kiln wall."

Psoli chuckled, bemused by the possibility. With a few parting words, he left. I indulged in a hot bath, letting the steam unwind my thoughts, and soon a servant came to summon me for dinner.

The meal was lavish, yet everyone picked at their food, minds clearly preoccupied with the mystery of the charcoal.

Conversations were sparse, each person absorbed in thoughts of how they might later connect with the soul within the charcoal.

After dinner, we sipped wine in silence until Psoli declared, "Let us begin."

The séance room was cloaked in an eerie ambiance, the flickering candlelight casting shadows that danced across the walls. As we gathered around the table, each person adopted their own method to connect with the soul they believed was encased in the charcoal. Some closed their eyes, whispering incantations, while others fixed their gaze intently on the blackened wood. Gan Mins paced restlessly in the corner, his movements as enigmatic as the task at hand.

Feeling somewhat out of place, I observed the proceedings, knowing I lacked the skills of a medium. I attempted to focus my thoughts, but the effort yielded nothing. Resigned, I watched the experts at work, hoping they might succeed where I could not.

Time seemed to stretch, the moments heavy with anticipation. Suddenly, two participants turned ashen and bolted from the room. Moments later, the sound of retching echoed from the hallway. Sir Psoli's voice broke the tension, murmuring with conviction, "There is a soul here. I can sense it."

The others nodded, affirming their shared intuition. Yet, intuition alone was insufficient; contact was needed to draw any meaningful conclusion.

The two who had left rejoined us, their faces pale and drawn, breathing heavily as they resumed their attempts. But as an hour slipped by with no tangible result, impatience crept over me. I quietly rose and moved to a corner, observing the scene with mounting skepticism. Could these disparate methods truly bridge the divide between the living and the spectral?

Three hours had passed since we began, and still, there was no breakthrough. Frustration gnawed at me, but leaving felt wrong—I was the catalyst for this gathering. Just as I was contemplating my next move, an unexpected disturbance shattered the stillness.

Gan Mins leapt to his feet, his expression a mix of emotions I couldn't quite decipher. It wasn't quite excitement, nor was it surprise, but something altogether different. Simultaneously, those touching the charcoal recoiled as if it had become searing hot or electrified, their hands jerking away.

For some, the force was so strong it propelled them backward, toppling chairs in their wake. The room erupted in chaos, screams mingling with the clatter of wood on the floor. It was clear that everyone had felt something profound and unsettling at the same moment.

I rushed forward, urgency in my voice. "What happened? What did you feel?"

The room's energy shifted, the air thick with a mixture of fear and awe. Each face reflected a shared experience, yet none spoke immediately. They were grappling with the ineffable, searching for words to describe what their senses had comprehended.

Sir Psoli was the first to find his voice, though it trembled slightly. "We touched the veil," he said, his eyes wide with wonder. "A force... a presence... it was undeniable."

The others nodded in agreement, still visibly shaken. In that charged atmosphere, it seemed we had indeed brushed against the boundary between our world and the next, leaving us with more questions than answers.

The room's tension hung thick as I asked, "What's wrong? What happened?"

CHAPTER 12

Soul Signals:
Communication Beyond the Flesh

No one answered.

The séance room was steeped in a heavy silence, punctuated only by the quick, uneven breaths of those gathered. Faces were etched with expressions I couldn't quite decipher—shock, awe, perhaps even fear. I hesitated, sensing that any question I posed might fall into the void of their collective, stunned consciousness. They were all deeply immersed in whatever revelation or sensation had just passed through them, leaving me as the outsider to their shared experience.

I couldn't help but feel the weight of the moment. These were individuals who had dedicated their lives to the study of the soul, and if anyone could bridge the chasm between our world and the ethereal, it would be them. Even without any personal sensory confirmation, I trusted their instincts and expertise.

My mind was a whirlwind of thoughts, trying to grasp the enormity of what was happening. The concept of souls communicating with the living was both thrilling and terrifying, a profound mystery of existence that defied logic and yet seemed so tantalizingly possible in this charged atmosphere.

As I attempted to voice my confusion again, the séance room was abruptly filled with the cacophony of barking dogs. The sound was jarring, slicing through the tension like a knife. It wasn't just a single bark, but a chorus from at least half a dozen dogs, their cries coming from various directions before converging at the door, accompanied by the frantic scratching of claws on wood.

The noise heightened the already surreal atmosphere. The dogs were clearly in a state of agitation, desperate to enter the room. I couldn't contain my bewilderment any longer and exclaimed, "Oh my God! What is happening?"

Gan Mins, breaking his silence, suggested letting the dogs in. Sir Psoli hesitated momentarily, then agreed. I moved to open the door, only to be halted by Psoli's urgent command to wait. He joined me swiftly, and before opening the door, he called out to the dogs, his voice firm yet soothing, quieting them with familiar commands.

Once calm prevailed, he opened the door cautiously. The first to burst through were two Dobermans, their movements sleek and purposeful as they bounded onto the table, growling menacingly at the charcoal. They were followed by a wolf dog, a sheepdog, a boxer, and two dachshunds, each displaying an uncharacteristic aggression towards the inanimate object.

The boxer, typically calm, was particularly fierce, its growls resonating with an intensity that made my skin prickle. Even the dachshunds, normally gentle due to their size, were now relentless, pawing at the table's edge and adding their snarls to the chorus.

Confounded by their behavior, I turned to Sir Psoli. "Sir, what's happening with these dogs?" I asked, my voice tinged with unease.

He gestured for silence, focusing intently on the dogs, who seemed to be reacting to some invisible force emanating from the charcoal. The others in the room shared knowing glances, their expressions indicating an understanding that eluded me.

Minutes ticked by, and gradually, the dogs' agitation subsided. They dismounted the table, pacing restlessly around the room, their earlier frenzy replaced by a lingering unease.

Under Sir Psoli's command, the dogs settled into obedient silence, their earlier frenzy replaced by a calm that seemed almost surreal. Yet, the quiet that enveloped the séance room only intensified the uncanny atmosphere, a tension that seemed to hum just beneath the surface.

Psoli's voice broke the silence, his tone probing yet gentle. Ash, I definitely sensed a presence just now. Did you experience anything similar?"

I shook my head, feeling somewhat out of step with the others. "No, it seemed as if everyone, dogs included, suddenly went berserk. Did you all sense the presence of a soul?"

Gan Mins nodded, his expression earnest. "Yes, I felt it," he affirmed.

Others echoed similar sentiments, some with fervent nods, others with quiet affirmations. One voice, belonging to the person who'd been physically jolted by his contact with the charcoal, was particularly emphatic. "I strongly felt it— right here!"

Their conviction left me baffled, prompting me to ask for clarity. "Can someone explain more specifically? What exactly did you feel?"

My request seemed reasonable to me, but it was met with looks of surprise and, from some, a touch of pity. Gan Mins opened his mouth as if to speak, but only sighed, a sound steeped in resignation. Psoli's gaze was both understanding and sympathetic, as if he was about to impart a difficult truth.

His voice was gentle as he approached, placing a reassuring hand on my shoulder. "It's not something that can be easily put into words, Ash. It's an elusive sensation, something that suddenly feels present. It's intangible—a fleeting, ethereal experience. Trying to describe it is like trying to catch smoke with your bare hands."

I chuckled, a mix of frustration and amusement bubbling up. "Really? In ancient eastern tales, the appearance of spirits is often marked by a chill—a wind that makes your hair stand on end."

Gan Mins interjected with a wry smile, "Perhaps that's because Orientals are particularly sensitive. "The room was thick with tension, a palpable charge in the air as Gan Mins' words echoed with a sharp edge of sarcasm. I shot back swiftly, "If you can't even articulate your feelings, how can you expect others to believe in the existence of ghosts?"

Psoli shook his head slowly, a knowing smile playing on his lips. "That's where you're mistaken. Sensing the presence of souls is a deeply personal experience. We don't need others to believe us, nor do we have to present tangible evidence to convince them."

I challenged him, "So, by your logic, the study of souls will forever remain obscure?"

Gan Mins chuckled, a sound that dripped with condescension. "Of course. What do you think spiritualism is? Some elementary curriculum?"

His words stung, leaving me momentarily speechless. Yet, as my anger subsided, I had to concede there was a sliver of truth in his argument. The study of souls is an arcane science, shrouded in mystery, concerned more with the nuances of the mind and fleeting sensations than concrete facts.

Spiritualism, like Einstein's theory of relativity, is a domain reserved for the few who dare to tread its enigmatic paths. It thrives in its obscurity, untouched by the need for widespread acceptance.

I pressed on, "What, then, is the nature of the ghost you claim to sense?"

Psoli spoke first, his voice steady. "I feel him, here, in this piece of charcoal. I am certain."

His gaze swept the room, meeting nods of agreement. The man with his hand resting on the charcoal added, "Indeed, he's in there. But why doesn't he reveal himself?"

I bypassed the question. "The key point is everyone agrees there's a soul in this charcoal. How do we communicate with it, extract information?"

Silence fell, thick and lingering, until Psoli murmured, "I believe he sent us a signal, one that only allows us to sense his presence, nothing more."

I suggested, "Typically, a soul communicates through the body of a medium."

Gan Mins interjected, "But if he's trapped in the charcoal, how can he inhabit any of us?"

I recalled Uber Dingle's words, unable to refute Gan Mins. Then Psoli remarked, "Humans' intuition is dull; dogs, however, are far more perceptive."

His words jolted me. "Are you suggesting that the dogs' strange behavior was in response to the soul's signal?"

Psoli nodded confidently. "What other explanation is there?"

I glanced at the dogs, their unusual behavior lending credence to his theory. "Dogs have senses far surpassing ours. Their sense of smell is beyond our comprehension, and their hearing—"

The room was alive with an undercurrent of revelation, a shared realization that sparked like a flint igniting tinder. Observing the dogs' peculiar behavior, I was struck by an epiphany. "Dogs' senses are undoubtedly more acute than ours," I mused aloud. "Their sense of smell is extraordinary, and their hearing—"

Then, like a bolt of lightning, clarity struck. At that exact moment, Gan Mins exclaimed, "Oh my God, the dogs' hearing!"

The atmosphere shifted instantly, a collective surge of excitement rippling through the group. We all knew it—dogs' hearing surpasses human capabilities significantly. Humans can hear frequencies up to 20,000 Hz, beyond which our ears register only silence. Yet, that silence is alive with sound, much like a world of melodies unreachable to the deaf.

Dogs, however, perceive a broader spectrum. They respond to frequencies humans cannot detect, guided by the silent call of a high-frequency whistle. To us, these whistles are mute, but to dogs, they sing commands.

Considering this, I recalled two critical observations: the strange patterns on Peter's X-ray, reminiscent of high-frequency waveforms; and the charcoal's peculiar readings at customs, hinting at similar frequencies.

With this realization, I shouted, "He's trying to communicate with us! He wants to speak!"

Gan Mins, ever the skeptic, retorted, "He's not trying. He already has!"

I was too elated to argue, acknowledging his point. "Yes, but he communicates through high-frequency sounds beyond our hearing. Your sensitivity catches only fleeting feelings, but the dogs hear it with clarity."

The room buzzed with agreement, a collective acknowledgment of the breakthrough in spiritualism—a soul reaching out, not through ethereal senses but tangible sound waves.

Psoli, overtaken by wonder, exclaimed, "What is he saying? I never imagined souls could speak. Why are human ears so inadequate?"

His frustration was palpable as he tugged at his ears, and I quickly reassured him, "Don't worry, sir. If he can produce sound, we can decipher his message."

Psoli challenged, "But how can we understand what we cannot hear?"

I hadn't solved the puzzle yet, but inspiration struck. "We can't hear it, but we can see it!"

Gan Mins scoffed, "Seeing sound? Really?"

His derision stoked a fire within me. I grinned, inches from his face, and retorted, "That's because you're too short-sighted! Sound can indeed be seen—we just need to visualize the waveform!"

In that moment, the promise of unraveling the soul's message felt within reach, a tantalizing mystery waiting to be decoded.

The room was charged with a palpable energy, a mix of exhilaration and frustration. Our collective excitement at discovering the sound emanating from the charcoal was tempered by the realization that it was a high-frequency sound beyond human hearing. Yet, when I proposed a solution, the mood shifted; a cheer rose among us.

Gan Mins stood there, blinking in silence, momentarily at a loss for words. Satisfied that I had finally gotten under his skin, I turned away, reaching into my briefcase and pulling out some crucial items. "Everyone, take a look at this."

I spread out the photos from Peter's lab, the ones with those peculiar irregular stripes, alongside the sound wave readouts from the customs inspection. The analysis revealed high-frequency sounds embedded within the charcoal.

The group, including a begrudging Gan Mins, crowded around to examine the evidence. The waveforms from the inspection mirrored those in the photos—unpredictable in their fluctuations yet seemingly grouped into four distinct patterns.

Though I considered publishing these waveforms, the complexities of publication processes dissuaded me. To the untrained eye, these waveforms appeared as nothing more than erratic lines, devoid of meaning.

Gan Mins sighed, a rare moment of reflection. "Humans pride themselves on their intellect, yet our abilities are limited. Dogs perceive sounds beyond our range, and moths communicate through high-frequency waves over miles, while we stand clueless before these signals. It's a humbling realization."

A seemingly unassuming man, silent until now, spoke up. "He communicates in a language of monosyllables."

Intrigued, I asked, "How do you know?"

He explained, "I specialize in languages, using a modern method that identifies linguistic characteristics through sound wave patterns."

His revelation heightened the tension in the room. Psoli, barely containing his excitement, urged him, "Tell us, what did he say?"

The man offered a rueful smile. "I can only discern four syllables, four monosyllables. They might form a meaningful sentence or be mere sounds without meaning. No one can reconstruct speech accurately from sound wave patterns alone."

The room fell into a contemplative silence, the mystery deepening even as the pieces began to align. We were on the brink of a breakthrough, yet the enigma of the monosyllabic message lingered, challenging us to look beyond what we could hear.

The room was thick with frustration, each face reflecting a shared sense of helplessness. But then, a thought sparked in my mind, and I waved my hand with newfound determination. "I know someone who can identify sounds from waveforms!"

Eyes turned toward me, a mix of skepticism and curiosity. I recounted what Peter had once mentioned—a person capable of discerning music from the waveform displayed on an oscilloscope.

Reactions were mixed—some chuckled, others shook their heads in disbelief, but one voice rose above the murmur: "Invite him! Perhaps he can help. Who is this person?"

Psoli interjected, "Ash, find this person!" Despite my confidence, I had no idea who this waveform wizard might be. Peter's tale could well be myth or legend.

Nonetheless, I resolved to contact Peter. "I need a phone," I announced.

"Use the one in my study," Psoli offered promptly.

I exited the séance room, pausing at the door. "Keep at it. We're on the brink of something big."

With nods of agreement echoing behind me, I closed the door. A servant appeared, and I requested to be led to the study.

The study, sprawling and lined with bookshelves, exuded an air of scholarly pursuit. I didn't need to inspect closely to recognize volumes dedicated to spiritual research. Yet, it was the central decor that amused me—a collection of

Taoist talismans, framed in pure silver, used for summoning spirits and exorcising ghosts. A touch of the mystical amidst the academic, it seemed Psoli had a flair for dramatic irony.

I approached the phone, the weight of our task heavy on my mind. The path ahead was uncertain, but each step brought us closer to unlocking the spectral secrets hidden within the charcoal.

Seated at the grand desk, my fingers hovered over the phone, pausing to collect my thoughts in the quiet that enveloped the room. The journey thus far had been a labyrinth of bizarre twists, leading me to the discovery of a soul within a piece of charcoal. This ethereal entity, invisible and intangible, was unlike anything I'd encountered, yet it emitted high-frequency sound waves—a potential breakthrough in proving contact between the living and the spectral.

I pondered the implications while waiting for the call to connect. If souls truly existed and could communicate with the living, what impact would that have on our understanding of life and consciousness? Why had these high-frequency signals gone unnoticed for so long? Could it be that the soul within the charcoal possessed unique properties that defied our comprehension?

The phone rang, interrupting my musings. I picked up the receiver, and Peter's voice crackled across the line. "Hello, who is it?"

"Peter, it's Ash!" I replied, my voice tinged with urgency.

"Ash! You're calling from London? What's so important?"

"I need to ask about someone. You once mentioned a person who could identify music from waveforms—mistaking the William Tell Overture for a pastoral symphony?"

Peter hesitated, clearly puzzled by my long-distance inquiry. "Yes, there's such a person."

"Who is he? How can I reach him? I need his expertise."

Peter sighed, "Ash, you're a bit of an oddball, but this guy takes the cake!"

I waved away his concerns, "It's fine, just tell me more about him. I can handle all sorts of oddballs."

"Well," Peter continued with a hint of amusement, "he fancies himself a genius, is interested in everything under the sun, and claims to be a master of deduction. He's prone to wild fantasies—like the time he insisted he found aliens living in a strange suburban house and claimed to have fought two of them. One supposedly had only half a face—"

Before he could finish, I exclaimed, "Oh my God!"

Peter paused, taken aback by my outburst. "What's gotten into you?"

I took a deep breath, "I know this person. His name is Harlan Brown!"

"Yes, that's him," Peter confirmed, sounding relieved. "You know him, great. You can reach out to him directly. I'd rather not deal with his madness."

"Thanks, Peter," I replied, hanging up with a wry smile. The prospect of engaging with Harlan was daunting. His eccentricity was legendary, and I wasn't particularly eager to dive into his chaotic world. Yet, his unique ability to interpret sound waveforms was precisely what I needed.

As I asked the operator to connect me with Harlan, I strategized on how to navigate our impending conversation. Engaging with him would require a delicate balance—enough information to pique his interest, but not so much that he'd entangle himself inextricably in the mystery.

I hesitated, my hand hovering over the phone. Calling Harlan directly might plunge me into an endless cycle of tangents and distractions. His mind was a labyrinth, and the last thing I needed was to get lost in it. Realizing this, I quickly canceled the call with the operator and made my way back to the séance room.

As I entered, it was clear that Psoli and his team hadn't progressed much in my absence. "How is it going?" Psoli asked, his eyes filled with anticipation.

"We can reach him," I replied, "but it's best if I go to him. He's in the city where I live."

The room filled with murmurs of surprise and intrigue. I could see the eagerness in their eyes, the desire to be part of this next step. I quickly added, "There's no need for everyone to come along. I'll present the waveforms to him first. If he's truly capable, we can plan our next steps."

Psoli's gaze shifted to the piece of charcoal on the table. "Will you take our friend with you?"

I understood his hesitation. This piece of charcoal was more than just an object; it was the culmination of his life's work. "I'll leave it here. Just ensure it's kept safe."

Psoli beamed with relief, expressing his gratitude. "Of course! We'll handle it with the utmost care."

I assured him, "I'll be in touch as soon as I have news." With that, I gathered the photos and waveform recordings, tucking them securely into my briefcase. "I'll rest now and head out in the morning."

Psoli nodded, though his focus was already back on the charcoal. "We won't lose a moment. You wouldn't understand, but this is too important."

I refrained from arguing, knowing their dedication was unwavering. I retired to the room prepared for me, though sleep was elusive. My mind raced with possibilities and plans.

At dawn, I packed my belongings and prepared to leave. I intended to bid farewell to Psoli, but the servant stopped me. "The lord instructed that Mr. Morris need not disturb him. They are not to be interrupted."

I chuckled at their single-mindedness. "And they starved too?" I asked with a smile.

The servant returned a wry grin. "There's a small opening for meals."

Shaking my head at their devotion, I left Sir Psoli's stately home and headed straight to the airport. Once home, I recounted the entire saga to Flora, detailing the strange happenings and my plans with Harlan. Her eyes widened at the tale, and together we pondered the next steps in this ever-evolving mystery.

CHAPTER 13

The Soul's Plea

Flora's excitement was contagious as she urged, "What are we waiting for? Let's find Chen Harlan!"

"Of course," I nodded, "though handling him without losing my patience will be the real challenge."

Flora chuckled, "Just present the waveforms as a test of his skills. He'll be eager to prove himself and decipher the sounds for you."

"Brilliant idea!" I laughed, picking up the phone to contact Harlan.

When he answered, a familiar impatience colored his voice. "Wait a minute, I can guess who you are!"

I bit back my irritation as he rattled off names. Finally, I interjected, "Enough with the guessing game!"

"Ah, Ash, I knew it was you!" he exclaimed, as if he'd solved a great mystery.

I sighed, "Yes, it's me. Listen, are you free? I need your special expertise."

He cut me off, "I have many special abilities. By the way, I was just about to find you. Do you remember the man with the half face? Along with him, there are some mysterious figures, and I'm almost certain they are invaders from outer space..."

"Come over," I interrupted, steering the conversation back on track. "I have something to show you. Drive safely."

I hung up before he could derail the conversation again, knowing he'd soon be on his way. I prepared the photos and waveform records on the table and awaited his arrival.

True to form, Harlan arrived within ten minutes, bursting through the door with pointed accusations. "It's rude to hang up like that!"

I smirked, "And storming in like this is polite?"

He blinked, then shrugged it off. "Alright, so what is it?"

I wasted no time, pushing the waveforms toward him. "What do you make of these sounds?"

He glanced at the papers, his expertise evident. "High-frequency waveforms. There's no sound here!"

"Impressive," I acknowledged, watching his demeanor shift to one of pride. "You identified it immediately."

Pleased with himself, Harlan puffed up. "This is nothing for me. Now, about that half-faced man—"

I cut him short again, pointing out the four distinct waveforms. "These represent four different sounds, possibly a sentence."

His eyes widened, and he hesitated, seemingly grappling with the task. "What do you mean?"

I reassured him, "Help me solve this, and I'll tell you everything about the half-face. I've figured it out."

"Really?" he exclaimed, lowering his voice conspiratorially. "Which planet are they from?"

Feigning intrigue, I replied, "A small, unimpressive one, orbiting a larger planet."

His excitement was palpable as he leaned forward, focused on the waveforms. "What do you need?"

"I need to know what these sounds are. Linguists suggest they might form a coherent message," I explained.

Harlan's bluntness took me by surprise as he dismissed the linguist's theory with an indelicate remark, "This linguist must have grown up eating shit!"

I was taken aback, "Why would you say that?"

He shot back, "Because if it's a high-frequency sound wave, how can it possibly be a language outside the range of human hearing?"

I decided to steer the conversation back on track. "Let's not worry about that. If we adjust these waveforms to a lower frequency, bringing them into the range audible to the human ear, what kind of sound do we get?"

His curiosity piqued, Harlan asked, "Is this a secret code or something?"

Exasperated by his endless questions, I replied, "Just focus on identifying it. If you can figure it out, great. If not, let's move on."

Harlan's eyes narrowed with determination. "Of course, I can recognize it!"

With that, he bent over the waveforms, his earlier skepticism giving way to concentration. His unique expertise was undeniable, and despite his eccentricities, I knew he was the right person for this task. It was only a matter of time before he unraveled the mystery behind the ghostly sounds.

Harlan's analytical process was both fascinating and frustrating. As he deciphered the waveforms, I felt a mix of anticipation and impatience. His interpretations were intriguing, yet they seemed to lead nowhere.

"The first syllable sounds like 'L' from 'let'," he explained, adding a nasal "E" sound to demonstrate potential words like "let" or "led."

When he asked if he was correct, I could only shrug. "I don't know, that's why I asked you."

He moved on to the second syllable with confidence, identifying it as a heavier, muddled "T," akin to "te" or "ti." Again, I was left without clarity, though his ability to translate the waveform into sound was impressive.

For the third syllable, he described a peculiar sound, mimicking it by blowing into his fist. "It's like air rushing through a narrow channel," he said, struggling to articulate it. Flora suggested it might be an "M" sound, which Chen quickly affirmed, likening it to the word "me" that peaks in waveforms.

His insights were remarkable, yet the words seemed disjointed, lacking any coherent meaning. When I asked about the final syllables, he confidently identified them as "OU" and "T," resulting in sounds like "out."

He then put down the paper and looked at me with a mysterious expression on his face, saying, "That person with half the face..."

Harlan's insistence on discussing the "man with half a face" was becoming tiresome. I interrupted him, hoping to set the record straight. "His face was burned in an accident. It's really that simple!"

Harlan reacted as if I'd stepped on his toes. "But you said they're from a planet!"

"Yes, from Earth. The same planet where we live." I clarified, watching his expression shift through a spectrum of emotions.

His face flushed with frustration, and I quickly added, "There's something unusual about them, but you have to let me explain without interruptions."

Harlan's demeanor softened slightly, and he turned to Flora for support. "Flora, if you weren't here, I'd have decked him!"

Flora played along, "He probably deserves it!"

This seemed to appease him, and with a sense of satisfaction, he allowed me to continue. I urged him to sit and explained the situation as straightforwardly as possible: there was a ghost trapped in a piece of charcoal, and these high-frequency sound waves were its attempt at communication.

Harlan listened intently, his eyes widening in disbelief. Once I finished, I asked, "Now that you know the story, can you decipher what Mr. Ghost is saying with these sounds?"

He sat in silence for a moment, absorbing the information. Then, with renewed focus, he picked up the waveform papers again, scrutinizing them carefully. His earlier bravado was replaced with a genuine curiosity and determination to solve the mystery.

After a thoughtful pause, he began testing different combinations of sounds, each attempt getting us closer to understanding the ghost's message. Finally, with a look of revelation, Harlan exclaimed, "I think I've got it. The soul might be saying 'Let me out.' It fits the waveforms perfectly!"

The ghost's plea, hidden in the sound waves, was a revelation. It opened the door to understanding its presence and perhaps even freeing it from its confinement within the charcoal. This breakthrough was a significant step forward in our peculiar investigation.

The shock of hearing "Let me out" was indescribable. These words echoed in my mind, a plea from the soul of Asim Dingle trapped within the charcoal. I imagined him crying out for years, desperately seeking release. The weight of such a revelation was profound, and it left me feeling both awed and unsettled.

Harlan watched me, his eyes wide with a mix of curiosity and concern as he noticed how pale I'd become. I managed to speak, my voice trembling slightly, "I believe we have understood this sentence: 'Let me out.' It must be that."

Silence enveloped us as we absorbed the enormity of the discovery. The phrase "Let me out" was not just a sentence; it was a glimpse into the mysterious realm that transcends life and death. It was a reflection of the human soul's deepest mysteries, now laid bare before us.

After a long pause, Flora broke the silence, "This reminds me of a Western myth."

Harlan quickly interjected, "Yes, like a devil trapped in a bottle!"

I chuckled despite myself, "Let's not complicate things further with myths. We need to focus on confirming that these high-frequency sound waves truly represent a language."

Harlan asserted confidently, "There's no doubt about it."

Taking a deep breath, I continued, "We shouldn't stop at 'Let me out.' We need to communicate more, but deciphering waveforms syllable by syllable could take days. Is there a more efficient method?"

Harlan rolled his eyes, "What can be a better way?"

Flora's suggestion sparked an idea. "The pronunciation of the 26 letters corresponds to distinct waveforms. With these, we could construct entire sentences."

Harlan's excitement was palpable. "Where's the ghost? Let me ask!"

I cautioned, "Be respectful when you address him."

Harlan shrugged, "Fine, a soul then. Where's the soul? In the charcoal, right?"

I sighed, knowing that despite his quirks, Harlan was indispensable. "The charcoal is with a group of spiritualists in London."

"Tell them to bring it here!" Harlan insisted.

Though his words were often brusque, I agreed with him this time. "I'll call Sir Psoli. He'll be thrilled. We also need a high-frequency sound wave detector."

Harlan patted his chest with confidence. "I have one! But it's quite large and not easy to transport."

Flora interjected, "Then let's not move it. We can all gather at your place."

Harlan's eyes lit up with excitement, and he looked at me expectantly. Acknowledging his contribution, I said, "Harlan, this is your time to shine."

He beamed, "Too bad that half-faced man wasn't an alien!"

Flora added wisely, "But being the first to communicate with a soul is an even greater achievement. The mysteries of life are more compelling than those of the universe."

Harlan, buoyed by the compliment, hummed an incomprehensible tune as he left, a spring in his step.

Taking the opportunity, I went to the study to call Sir Psoli and share our findings. His voice echoed with excitement, "Oh my God! Oh my God!"

"Enough with the 'my God'! Just bring the charcoal, and anyone interested can join," I urged.

Sir Psoli agreed enthusiastically. I anticipated a small group, but to my surprise, everyone was eager to come along. We all made our way to Harlan Brown's residence.

Harlan's ancestral home, a sprawling expanse filled with endless corridors and hidden chambers, was the perfect backdrop for our clandestine gathering. We convened in his "sound room," a place steeped in mystery, to conduct the experiment that could alter our understanding of life and death.

The room was charged with an air of anticipation, akin to the moment before a storm breaks over the horizon.

With reverence, we placed the ancient piece of charcoal upon the detection device. Harlan, his hands steady and precise, adjusted the instrument, setting the stage for what could be a monumental discovery.

The recording apparatus lay poised, its pen hovering over the roll of paper awaiting waveforms that might defy logic. The tension in the room was palpable. I inhaled deeply and addressed the presence we hoped to contact, "Mr. Dingle, if the legends are true, and as your ancestor Uber Dingle chronicled, you possess an uncanny awareness of the world beyond your confines. Can you hear us? Are you there?"

Silence enveloped us, thick and almost oppressive. Each second stretched into eternity as we exchanged anxious glances, beads of sweat beginning to dot foreheads.

Then, as if responding to an unspoken call, the pen jerked into motion. A series of waveforms danced across the paper, each curve a testament to the unseen. Harlan's voice broke the silence, a triumphant shout, "Yes! Yes!"

The room erupted in a cacophony of disbelief and exhilaration. Gan Mins whispered, awe-struck, "Conversing with a soul... it's beyond imagination!"

Sir Psori, his cheeks flushed with excitement, declared, "This is the moment I've awaited my entire life!"

I pressed on, emboldened by the response, "Mr. Dingle, we know you're within the charcoal. Do you wish for us to release you—"

Before I could complete my thought, the pen trembled with an almost supernatural energy, etching an intricate pattern of waveforms across the page. They conveyed a message so urgent, so primal, that it bypassed the need for Harlan's translation: "Let me out."

I voiced the spectral plea to the assembled group, their eyes widening, oscillating between fear and an insatiable curiosity. "Mr. Dingle," I urged, the room hanging on the precipice of revelation, "tell us how to set you free."

We collectively held our breath, the air thick with anticipation, waiting for the enigmatic response that could unravel the mysteries binding us to this moment.

CHAPTER 14

The Experience of Asim Dingle

In the days that followed, our small group became a collective of insomniacs, driven by an insatiable need to communicate with Asim Dingle. Meals were forgotten, the concept of sleep became foreign, and we found ourselves engrossed in conversations that stretched the limits of our understanding.

Initially, our exchanges were limited to a mere handful of simple sentences each day. But as time progressed, our proficiency grew. The dialogues became more intricate, allowing us to delve into the complexities of our enigmatic situation.

Five months passed in this feverish state. During this time, we abandoned the comforts of everyday life, taking up residence on the floor of Harlan's modest home. Grooming fell by the wayside, and we transformed into a band of modern-day savages, consumed by our quest for answers.

Even in sleep, the recording pen would stir, inscribing waveforms on endless rolls of paper. We lost count of how many we used, each roll a testament to our relentless pursuit of Asim Dingle's story.

Throughout this period, we pieced together the narrative of Asim Dingle's journey to Charcoal Gang and Ashfield Valley. I meticulously documented his experiences, creating what could be considered the most extensive confession from a soul to the living in history. The dialogue unfolded in a question-and-answer format, preserving the authenticity of our interactions.

The concept of "spirit" remained a profound mystery, defying the conventional bounds of human language. How does an entity without form or ears hear? Yet, somehow, it does. Our vocabulary falters at such enigmas, forcing us to stretch the limits of expression.

I began with a simple inquiry: "Mr. Dingle, are you trapped within the charcoal?"

"Yes, for a long time. Since entering, I have been unable to leave. Let me out!"

I responded with a helpless smile, "We don't fully understand. In the charcoal? What does that mean? How can we help you escape?"

"In the charcoal, just as a person might be in the air, I am trapped. I want out!"

"How can we release you? By breaking the charcoal?"

"No! Do not break it. If you do, I will dwell in one of the fragments."

"You mean, even if shattered into countless pieces, you're still within the charcoal? Even in the tiniest particle?"

"Yes!"

I sighed, perplexed by his predicament. "Isn't that a worse fate?"

After a pause, he replied, "Not necessarily. For me, large and small are indistinguishable."

(We struggled to comprehend how "big" and "small" could be the same.)

"Then tell us, what should we do?"

"I don't know."

(That he himself lacked the knowledge to escape was a bizarre revelation.)

Cautiously, I asked, "Are you saying you may never be able to leave the charcoal?"

"No! No! There must be a way. Uber Dingle entered a tree and managed to leave."

"How did he manage that?"

A long silence followed before he began again, "Let us start from the beginning. Do you know why I went to Ashfield Valley?"

"I have an idea. Was it for the treasure, or to uncover the secrets of life in pursuit of eternity?"

"Both, though my heart yearned more for the latter. I left without regrets. It surprised me, yet seemed natural. When I reached Ashfield Valley, I was too late. The tree that Uber Dingle inhabited had been felled. The stump remained, marked by symbols on the map. I found it with ease but couldn't determine if Uber Dingle's presence lingered within the stump or the severed trunk."

"An impossible determination. So you—"

"I remained focused by the stump, trying to connect with Uber, but felt nothing. So, I ventured to the Charcoal Gang to locate the cut trunk."

"Indeed, I know you went to see Uncle Four. Yet, you insisted on entering the charcoal kiln—"

"I had no choice but to enter. After my request was denied, it was imperative to enter the kiln."

"Mr. Dingle, I must understand your reasoning. Were you aware of the peril in entering the charcoal kiln?"

"Yes."

"And did you realize it might cost you your life?"

"I know, the moment I stepped into the charcoal kiln, it wasn't a question of 'might' lose my life—it was a certainty."

"Then why did you make such a resolute decision? Did Uber Dingle finally impart some enlightenment to you?"

"No, there was no epiphany from Uber Dingle before I entered the kiln. You wonder why I did it—it's because I had already grasped the essence of life."

"I'm sorry, I don't follow. You say you know life, but does that mean one must forsake life upon understanding it?"

"One must forsake the body."

"I still don't comprehend. For most, to abandon the body is to abandon life itself. I must ask again: Does knowing life compel one to abandon the body? Or, does it mean finding one's own path to death?"

(After posing this question, there was an unnerving silence. It stretched so long that we feared we might never receive another message. But eventually, the communication resumed. Clearly, this question challenged even a soul's understanding.)

"No, I think it varies. Not everyone is afforded the chance to step into what comes after the body, which is death. My understanding is incomplete, as I've been confined to the charcoal, with no opportunity to learn of other such experiences. But for me, prior to entering the kiln, I felt no attachment to my then-life form. I was certain of transitioning into another form."

"What gives you such certainty?"

"You've read the records of Uber Dingle. It was his writings that inspired me."

"What led you to detach from your previous life form? We all exist in this form."

"Too brief, too painful! Sir, had I not shifted my existence at that moment, would we be conversing now?"

"That's not necessarily the case. I've met your wife—she's in good health."

"Really? And how many years does she have left?"

(I was at a loss. By Asim's reckoning, how long does the "first form of life" last? A century at most.)

"Please, recount what transpired after you entered the charcoal kiln. Let's set aside the complexities of life forms for now. It's a challenging concept for us all."

"Indeed, it's not easily grasped. Few can comprehend it, which is why many are consumed by futile pursuits in such a fleeting existence. They expend immense effort on these endeavors. It's truly pitiable!"

"Please, tell me what happened after you entered the charcoal kiln!"

"As soon as I leaped into the charcoal kiln, I found myself crashing into its center, where no wood lay, just an ominous void. The distance from the top was significant, and when I hit the ground, a searing pain shot through my legs. I suspected my bones had fractured. At the same moment, my body pitched to the side, colliding with a stack of timber. The wood toppled over, burying me beneath its weight."

"Hold on a moment. Fernsby and Bian claim that as soon as you entered the kiln, Uncle Four commanded the fire to be lit, and Bian Five plunged in to rescue you almost immediately. They said it took less than half a minute."

"I believe it scarcely took half a minute, but for the extraordinary transference of thought, half a second suffices. What was I recounting? Ah, yes, the wood pile crashed upon me, inflicting excruciating pain. It was at that moment, in an ephemeral second, that I heard it. I say 'heard,' though I'm uncertain if it was truly auditory."

"I am only certain that a voice declared to me: 'You are here! Finally, my descendant has come to witness my records!' In haste, I cried out: 'Uber Dingle!' The exchange was fleeting, yet I sensed he imparted much to me."

"What were his words?"

"He affirmed the correctness of my decision. He explained that a soul can inhabit any object. For years, he existed within a tree and now could depart. He warned that leaving an object is challenging, and he was uncertain of the consequences if a soul does not first enter an object—the soul might dissipate, cease to exist, which he opposed."

"Did you see him?"

"I saw nothing. By then, the kiln was a maelstrom of flames and thick smoke. My entire being was engulfed in an agony I'd never known. Yet, the pain was fleeting. Perhaps I clutched a piece of wood tightly at that moment. Abruptly, the torment vanished. Though the fire roared, the smoke billowed, and the flames encircled me, I felt no pain. My soul had successfully severed from my corporeal form, and I laughed."

"That's a remarkable achievement. What followed?"

"Once the fire subsided, I found myself amidst countless fires, enclosed in a space I couldn't escape. Despite this, I felt serene, free of desire or discomfort. I lost track of time until someone eventually released me from that confinement. Through conversation, I discovered I resided within a piece of charcoal."

"I apologize for my blunt question. Given the small size of the charcoal, you must have endured years of confinement. Was it painful?"

"You misunderstand. Regardless of how minuscule the charcoal is, even if it were the size of a mustard seed, it represents the entire universe to me. Let me explain with numbers: I am zero. Any number, no matter how small, is infinitely larger than zero. If a fraction's denominator is zero, the result is infinite, regardless of the numerator."

(Gan Mins posed the next question.)

"If so, why do you plea to 'let me out'? Isn't possessing the entire universe splendid?"

"You are mistaken. I am not seeking rescue. I never perceive myself as caged. I simply aspire to transition into the third form of life. Uber Dingle conveyed the sense of having transcended the second form to the third, and I too wish to move beyond the second form."

"Do you believe the third form will surpass the second?"

"It's not about superiority. It's the natural progression of life, and I intend to experience each stage as it unfolds."

"In your imagination, what does the third form of life entail?"

"I can't imagine it, just as I couldn't envision the second form while in the first."

"I believe we must address the most crucial question now: how can we help you leave this piece of charcoal?"

"I don't know."

"If you don't know, how can we 'let you out'? Surely, you must have some idea. Should we try smashing the charcoal?"

"You could attempt it, but I doubt it will work. Uber Dingle left the tree he inhabited when the wood was burned. Perhaps you could try burning the charcoal?"

This was Asim Dingle's own suggestion, and by this point, nearly three months had elapsed.

We exchanged uncertain glances, unable to make a swift decision. Of course, we all wished for Asim's life to advance to the "third form," but would incinerating the charcoal and reducing it to ashes truly liberate him?

If his words held true, that any object, no matter how minuscule, was infinitely large to him, then even the tiniest ashes could still serve as the vessel for his second form, making it impossible to "let him out."

After lengthy deliberation, we resumed our communication with Asim. His response was as follows:

"You must try. I will endeavor to inform you of the outcome. Don't worry; for you, situations may be 'good' or 'bad,' but for me, they are indistinguishable. Proceed with confidence!"

With Asim's reassurance, Harlan procured a large copper basin, placed the charcoal inside, and doused it with kerosene. Before igniting it, Gan Mins cautioned, "Be careful not to lose the ashes. If he can't leave yet and resides in a tiny ash particle, we might still contact him. Don't squander this chance!"

We unanimously agreed, yet when the box of matches circulated among us, no one was willing to strike one. When the match returned to me for the third time, I forced a wry smile and said, "It seems I have no choice but to accept this responsibility."

Silence pervaded the group. Clearly, the reluctance stemmed from not knowing what would occur once the fire was lit.

I struck the match and held it to the kerosene-soaked charcoal, which ignited instantly.

As the charcoal blazed, Harlan positioned the high-frequency sound wave detector as close as possible, hoping to capture any final messages from Asim Dingle.

Yet the recording pen remained still.

Nearly everyone fixated on the burning charcoal, myself included. But I suspect no one truly knew what to anticipate. Were we expecting an apparition to emerge from the inferno? Unlikely. Yet within the shifting flames and the thick smoke coiling upward, did Asim's soul reside?

Fire and smoke are ethereal by nature. Could Asim Dingle's soul have ascended with them? Did his third form commence as the flames and smoke dispersed? However, fire and smoke are but transformations of air, which consists of molecules. Though air molecules are negligible to us, for

Asim Dingle, who equates to "zero," they represent "the entire universe." Thus, might his soul have entered an air molecule, seeking another life form?

As the charcoal burned, my thoughts were a turbulent mix of questions and possibilities. I imagine others felt the same, judging by their bewildered expressions.

After about ten minutes, the burning charcoal fractured into smaller pieces, continuing to smolder. Thirty minutes later, only a few tiny particles glowed red amidst the ashes. A few minutes more, and the charcoal had conclusively transformed into ashes.

Once the charcoal was consumed, it wasn't simply reduced to ashes; it also released gases—an illustration of the "law of conservation of matter." Apart from the ashes, substantial gas had escaped, irretrievable. This gas, largely carbon dioxide, contained impurities from the high-temperature charcoal.

As I pondered this, Harlan positioned the ashes near the detector. The recording pen remained silent. We waited, but no response came.

I broke the silence. "He's gone."

Psoli echoed, "Yes, he's gone."

I clarified, "I mean he's no longer here."

Gan Mins, puzzled, asked, "I don't understand—"

I explained, "I mean, he's no longer within this ash pile. He might have successfully transitioned into the third form of life, or perhaps he's entered a gas molecule. For him, a molecule is indistinguishable from a piece of charcoal!"

Silence enveloped us once more.

Psoli sighed after a pause, "In any case, we can no longer reach him."

I reminded them, "He promised to contact us and share insights, so—"

Several voices chimed in unison, "We still have to wait!"

Among those who insisted on waiting was Harlan Brown. He was adamant about maintaining hope for further contact with Asim Dingle's soul, which was crucial since everyone was waiting at his home.

The wait stretched into an agonizing duration. A month passed without a trace of Asim's presence, leading some to depart. After two months, more followed. By the third month, even Gan Mins and Psoli conceded defeat.

Only Harlan, Flora, and I remained, holding out for over another month, yet still without any sign.

That evening, the three of us gathered, and I said with a wry smile, "It seems there will be no further messages. Let's speculate on his current state."

Harlan mused, "Perhaps he left the charcoal only to become trapped within a gas molecule, drifting aimlessly, unable to reach us."

I added, "That's one possibility. Another is that he advanced to the third form of life, a state in which he cannot communicate with us."

Harlan nodded, "That's possible too."

Both of us had shared our thoughts, but Flora remained silent. We turned our attention to her.

Flora replied, "You want to know what I think?"

"Yes," Harlan encouraged.

"My view is rather bleak," Flora admitted.

Harlan quickly interjected, "Do you mean he's vanished, ceased to exist?"

Flora clarified, "No, I mean that Asim's soul, having once entered the charcoal post-mortem, has now left it."

Harlan, more anxious than I, asked, "Isn't that good? Why the pessimism?"

Flora reminded us, "Recall his reasoning for detaching from life: its brevity and its pain."

Harlan sighed, "Indeed, life is both short and painful."

Flora continued, "This is why I'm pessimistic. After leaving the charcoal, his soul may have entered the so-called third form, which could simply be inhabiting another body."

Our eyes widened in realization. "Reincarnation?" I suggested.

"Exactly," Flora confirmed.

Harlan and I were struck silent, grappling with the implications. "If that's true, wouldn't he face another short and painful life?" I asked.

"Precisely," Flora nodded. "That's what he desperately sought to avoid, in his quest for the eternity of life. But does such eternity exist? Or is it just an endless cycle of changing forms?"

Harlan and I shared a bitter laugh, contemplating the futility of escaping the body if it merely led back to the start. Is this truly the cycle? Or is the truth something else entirely?

No one—not even a soul—could provide answers. From that day forward, Asim Dingle's soul never reached out again. I remain in the dark about his fate, but I suspect it lies within one of our three theories.

Of course, a fourth possibility might exist, one so far beyond our comprehension that we can't even conceive of it.

(Later, in my search for understanding the mystery of the soul, I discovered profound and enlightening answers within Buddhist teachings. It was there that I found the path to liberation from the endless cycle of reincarnation—the way to truly attain eternity. However, the journey is deeply personal and transformative, one that cannot be fully conveyed in mere words. I encourage you to embark on your own quest, to discover your answers and forge your own path to enlightenment.)